RETURN TO BAREBACK RANGE

A Novel Set On The Prairies

by Frank Sol

CHAPTER ONE

The sudden flashing of red lights in Jesse Helmer's rear view mirror made him jerk upright in his seat and he spilled his *Coke* all over the front seat of the Chevy. "Damn it!" Jesse frantically tried to slow the old truck down and pull over, while at the same time, keeping his lap from being drenched. The Alberta highway could be a nightmare to drive in the middle of the night as there were no streetlights, and tonight the moon was not friendly enough to be out. He could hear the grinding of the last bits of gravel underneath his tires as the truck slowly came to a stop. "Shit," he muttered.

A bright light shone in Jesse's rear view mirror as the patrol car came to a gentle stop on the gravel behind him, and turned off its red lights. The bright spotlight mounted on the side of the door made him turn his head away, blinking. He just looked out at the road beneath the driver's side door.

In a matter of seconds, he heard footsteps slowly crunching the gravel as the cop approached the truck.

The first thing he saw was a pair of black boots. Jesse slowly lifted his head, looking up the length of the shadowy figure until his eyes rested on the spotlighted face of a police officer.

Constable Steven Danials was a big man, but well groomed with a dark moustache that seemed to dominate his square-jawed face. He filled out his regulation uniform in a solid fashion. He gave a start when he suddenly realized Jesse was staring at him. "License and registration," he said in his deep voice.

That snapped out Jesse out of his trance and he hastily fumbled around inside his jeans until he came up with his wallet. "Sure thing, Constable." Jesse reached in and then handed over his driver's license and registration. "But you know it's me," he said plaintively.

Danials' stern face studied over the documents and then Jesse's face, almost as if Jesse was a stranger to him. He then turned and slowly walked back towards his patrol car without saying a word.

Jesse's heart was beating fast at this point. *What is he doing?* He knew he had been speeding just a little bit, but he did not think it was a problem so far out in the country. *There's no body else on the roads at this time of the night. It's not like I'm speeding through Nanton!* As he sat there, trying to see what the constable was doing back at his car, all of a sudden the spotlight was turned off and then the car's headlights. Jesse blinked, trying to quickly adjust to the change.

Danials approached Jesse's truck again and stood at Jesse's window with his hands on resting on his belt. "I need you to exit the truck, Mister Helmer, but do it slowly, eh?" he said with almost a hint of nervousness in his voice.

Jesse was confused as to what was going on and started thinking about what Clint was going to have to say about this. *He's gonna kill me if I get his truck impounded.* Jesse opened the cab door slowly and the constable took a step back. *What's up with him?* Jesse then closed the door as softly as he could while still making the latch click shut.

Jesse stood there on the side of the highway and just stared silently at the other man in the dark. He could make out the constable's broad shoulders and the way his uniform pants clung to his legs.

Danials swallowed a couple of times and then he cleared his throat.

Jesse was really starting to wonder just what *he* was so nervous about.

Daniels's eyes darted down to Jesse's chest, then dipped to his crotch, and then back up to Jesse's face in a matter of seconds.

Jesse looked down at himself, wondering if he had spilled any of the *Coke* on his clothes, but they looked clean enough.

"Go around to the other side of the truck," Danials said in his authoritative tone and he pointed.

"Okay." Jesse started walking and heard the crunch of gravel as Danials followed behind him.

Jesse was now hesitantly standing next to the passenger's side door of his truck as Danials nervously twisted his head to look up and down the highway. *What's going on with him? Is this an arrest or is he gonna beat the shit out of me or something?*

When he was through looking up and down the highway, Danials cleared his throat again, and then he slowly sank down to his knees. He squatted there in front of Jesse's crotch and ever so slowly reached out his hand until he placed it gently on the front of Jesse's *Wranglers*.

Jesse jumped, in surprise, and Danials hastily pulled his hand back.

Silently, Danials' eyes quickly locked with Jesse's and then, once again, his hand reached out and laid itself against Jesse's fly and gently felt around for his penis.

Jesse felt himself tremble as the constable's hand found what it was seeking and began to rub through the fabric. Danials was staring hungrily at the bulge that was rapidly taking shape in Jesse's blue jeans.

Jesse could feel the nervous electricity that was coursing through his veins as his cock grew harder, but he just could not help himself. His throbbing cock had a mind of its own and he was powerless to resist.

Danials seemed to relax a little more as he realized that Jesse was also getting more and more excited by his actions. His moustache twitched a little and his tongue darted out to quickly lick his lips. He looked back and forth down the highway again from his squatting position, and then slowly pulled Jesse's zipper down.

Jesse groaned softly as his cock finally popped out of the fabric and lightly slapped the police officer on the check. The warmth of his skin was an incredible contrast from the night air. Jesse took a deep breath as he leaned back a few inches and watch his cock bob up and down in the dark.

Danials also started breathing more heavily and fell to his knees in the gravel. He reached his shaking hand up and slowly grasped Jesse's cock in his hand.

Jesse watched as his mouth slowly opened and his moustache came closer to the head of hiss cock. He leaned forward and slid Jesse's cock under his thick moustache and into his warm mouth.

"Oh my God!" Jesse gasped as Danials tightened his suction. The cop had slid his mouth down his shaft and all the way to his balls, even turning his head sideways to keep his *Stetson* from coming off. Jesse leaned against the side of the truck as Danials started moving his mouth up and down his shaft.

Danials placed his hands on Jesse's thighs and squeezed them tightly as he picked up motion.

Jesse could feel his spit dribbling down his balls as his mouth watered more. He moaned every couple of seconds as he got into what he was doing. Jesse moaned as well, enjoying ever lick from the officer's tongue.

After another minute of sucking, Danials slowly removed his mouth. He wiped the drool from the corners of his moustache and looked up at the other man. "I want you to do something for me," he said, quietly. He slowly stood up and brushed the dirt from the knees of his uniform pants. Jesse could see the bulge in the front of his uniform trousers quite plainly and his own cock bounced again in excitement. After doing another routine check of the area, the officer reached down and unbuttoned the top of his pants. He unzipped and peeled his trousers down slowly over his thick thighs and firm butt. His beautiful cock hung down along with his furry balls. "I think you know what to do."

Jesse reached out in excitement and took hold of the large piece of meat with his hand. "Wow," he murmured softly. *I never expected to see this side of the Constable. I don't know what's gotten into him...but I'm not gonna miss my chance at any of this.* He reached out his hand.

Danials let out a heartfelt sigh as Jesse rubbed his hand up and down the long, smooth shaft.

Then Jesse leaned down and put his tongue on the end of Daniels's cock and noticed the salty taste of his pre-cum.

The officer backed away and looked down at him. "I don't want you to do that," he said as he walked towards the side of the truck hood. He laid his hard cock against the warm hood of the truck and then leaned down until he was lying against the truck. His muscular, furry ass was the only thing exposed.

Jesse walked over and put his hand on Daniels's nice butt and rubbed it around.

"I want you to put that inside me." He looked over his shoulder at Jesse's still hard cock. "I want it so badly." Danials spit into his palm and reached around and grabbed Jesse's cock with the wet spit and rubbed it on. He repeated the spit shine until Jesse's dick was wet and dripping. "Okay, now put it in." He turned his head back towards the road.

Jesse slowly positioned himself behind him and put the head of his cock between his crack.

Danials tightened a little and then relaxed. He used one hand and guided Jesse into position. "Push in," he ordered.

"You got it, Constable." Jesse finally took a hold of the cop's thighs and pushed hard against him until the head slipped in. Danials gasped and tightened and then relaxed again. Jesse pushed gently and let Jesse's cock slide up inside his warm ass.

Jesse moaned softly. His insides felt like warm silk as he slide in and then pulled out slowly again, just to the head.

Danials relaxed completely and put his hands back on the hood. "Fuck me hard, son," he said as his voice cracked. "Fuck me good."

Jesse started moving in and out in a gentle motion. The heat of this cop's ass was driving him crazy and he had to practically stand on the tips of his toes to reach. Jesse loved the sound of flesh slapping against flesh and the sucking sound made as he slid in and out, loved the sound of Danials moaning and breathing heavily. Jesse moved in and out and his cock kept growing harder. Jesse knew that he other man could feel it because he started tightening up again. This made his even more crazy and he picked up his pace.

"Damn, son!" Danials gasped as Jesse ploughed into him with such force that Jesse's balls touched his own whenever he went all the way in. The sensation was incredible.

Jesse started feeling that excitement that he got in his balls whenever he beat off. Jesse's cock got so hard it started to hurt as he tensed up. "Shit! I'm gonna blow!" Jesse gasped.

"Go ahead, do it, boy!"

"Fuck, here it comes!" He cried out as he felt the cum work its way up his shaft. Jesse pounded it deep inside him and shot another spurt.

"Fucking yeah!" Danials shouted as he pushed back against Jesse.

Jesse slumped over and lay panting on Daniels's back. Both of them were both out of breath. The sweet scent of sweat hung in the night air.

Chapter Two

Jesse poured hot water from the kettle into two coffee mugs.

Clint stumbled into the kitchen, inhaling the scent of fresh-brewed coffee. The heels of his worn black boots clicked softly on the linoleum floor. "Well ain't you just the happy homemaker."

Jesse turned towards him with a happy smile on his face. "Morning, Clint. I thought you were gonna stay in bed all day."

"I've got chores to do," Clint grumbled as he picked up his mug and took a long swallow of the black liquid. "Though I doubt I've got the energy left for them after satisfying you this morning." His blue denim shirt was hanging open, unbuttoned.

"I didn't hear any complaining about the way we were riding each other earlier," Jesse replied with a grin. He leaned back against the counter, his hands stuffed into the front pockets on his tight blue jeans.

"You were really eager for it this morning. Shit, I didn't think you were going to let me go."

Jesse shrugged. "I was just horny."

"You're telling me. What brought all that on?"

Jesse smiled wryly. He took a drink of his coffee, savouring the hot, bitter taste of the liquid to buy time for him to collect his thoughts. "I had the strangest dream last night."

"Oh?' Clint poured himself a second mug of coffee. "What kind of dream?" He sat down at the table and began to button up his shirt.

"I dreamed that I was pulled over by Constable Danials."

Clint raised an eyebrow at that.

"And instead of giving me a ticket, he gave me a blow job."

Clint choked on his coffee. "Shit!" He coughed. "I've had the odd dream about the good constable...but nothing quite like that."

"You think there's any chance of it really happening?"

Clint shook his head. "Not likely," he muttered. "Danials likes to tease, but I've never heard even the smallest hint that he's got any interest in men."

"Damn," Jesse said regretfully.

"Damn," Clint agreed.

* * *

Jesse lifted the rail into place against the fence and held it steady while Clint hammered in nails. When it was secure enough, Jesse let it go and mopped sweat from his brow and then wiped his hand on his jeans. He adjusted his hat to better shield his eyes from the sun. "It's a scorcher," he commented. He had taken off his green t-shirt an hour ago and his hairy chest was damp with sweat.

"Yeah, but it's only gonna get hotter." Clint's denim shirt was half-unbuttoned.

"It's summer, isn't it?" Jesse paused to take a long look around at the prairie. It stretched to the horizons in all directions, with the Rocky Mountains rising off to the west. The natural beauty of the mountains never stopped grew old for him.

"Back to work then." Clint reached into the bed of the Chevy, selecting the next rail for the fence.

"Mmm," Jesse said as he took in the sight of those faded blue *Wranglers* stretching across his partner's ass. "Very nice."

"What's very nice?"

"Watching you bend over."

Clint turned his head. "Watching me do all the work, you mean."

"No, just watching you in general."

Clint straightened up and adjusted his own hat. He muttered something under his breath.

Jesse smiled. "I mean it, Clint."

Clint just shook his head and pulled a beer out of the cooler in the Chevy's cab. "Shit."

He's a man of few words. Jesse took a beer for himself and popped it open. "It's nice to be on the farm," he said. "You've got a great view of the Rockies."

"Always have. Hardly even notice them now." He eyed Jesse, licking his lips at the sight of Jesse's hairy chest.

Jesse did not even notice—he was used to Clint watching him. *How can you just forget about them?* "I envied you when I first came here. You have your own little world out here and you don't need anyone."

"I wouldn't say that."

Jesse smiled. "I mean you're not tied to the town. We go weeks without setting foot off the property." *A month or more at times.*

Clint kicked at a clod of dirt. "Never had much use for the town. Older I get, the less need there is to go there."

Jesse looked at him. "Do you regret choosing to stay here on the farm?" he asked suddenly.

Clint looked at him. "What?"

"Last summer, when your old pal Jason was here, do you have any regrets about not going away with him?"

"Hell no!" Clint replied immediately. "Never." He shook his head. "Fuck, Jesse, don't ever think shit like that. There's things I regret, sure, but staying here with you ain't one of 'em."

Jesse smiled. "Just checking."

"Let's get back to work." Clint finished his beer. "What Jason and I had was in the past. It's over and done with. He's gone back to his big house in Calgary. And I am here with you."

Jesse set his beer down. "That was quite a speech for you," he commented.

Clint snorted. "It's the simple truth." He reached for another fence rail. "Now give me a hand with this thing."

* * *

"You look tired."

"I *am* tired," Jesse answered from the chair. His worn brown boots were lying on the floor beside him. He felt as bedraggled as he no doubt looked.

"You worked hard on that fence." Clint stooped down and took hold of Jesse's hands. "Maybe too hard. You're not some teenaged kid." He rubbed at the hard calluses on his partner's hands.

"I know. But neither are you."

"I've been working this farm since I was a boy. I know my limits."

"So do I." Jesse shrugged. "It's also getting kind of late too, you know." A few seconds later, he stifled a yawn.

"Well, now. There's only one thing to do about that," Clint said with a playful twinkle in his eyes.

"And that would be what?" Jesse asked as he played along. He already had a hunch were Clint was going with this conversation. *Woo-hoo! I just hope I have the energy for it.*

Clint stood up, not letting go of Jesse's hands. He bent down and with a sudden jerk, he pulled the other man up and out of the chair and then draped him over his shoulder like some rolled-up carpet. "It's off to bed with you, mister," he chuckled as he carried the other man to the bedroom.

Jesse could not help but chuckle along with him, as he offered not even the slightest token of resistance. *He barely grunted when he did that!* Clint was nearly ten years old than Jesse. *Shit, he's as strong as an ox.*

Clint deposited him onto their bed a few moments later. He did not just throw Jesse onto the bed either, but laid him down in the bed as gently as if he was a basket full of eggs.

Clint reached down and unbuttoned Jesse's faded *Wranglers*. He pulled down the zipper and then started to pull the now loosened jeans down off his hips. Jesse had closed his eyes as he lay there content to let

Clint strip him down. He knew that he enjoyed it as much as the other man did.

Clint lifted his legs up and pulled his jeans off with ease. Then he leaned over and undid the bottom button of Jesse's denim shirt.

Jesse opened his eyes just in time for Clint to kiss him on the lips. It was a soft, gentle, and all too brief kiss.

Clint undid the next button on his shirt as he worked his way up to the top of his shirt. A kiss on the lips followed the undoing of each button.

Shit, now that's the way to undress a guy! Jesse thought. *How do I get this kind of service all the time?*

Eventually Clint ran out of buttons to undo, and the kissing stopped. Clint rolled him onto his left side as he slipped Jesse's right arm out of the right sleeve of his shirt. As soon as his arm was free, Clint kissed him on the lips again. All Jesse could do was sigh with delight as Clint rolled him onto his right side and repeated the kiss.

Jesse felt it as Clint yanked the shirttail from under his butt. He lay on the bed with only his white cotton briefs on while Clint removed his socks.

For a few minutes nothing happened. Jesse could not feel Clint touching any part of his body, nor could he feel any movement on the bed that might have suggested that he was climbing on to it. Jesse forced his eyes open, as curiosity got the better of him. He was greeted with the sight of Clint standing before him striped down to his white boxers, and smiling. *Apparently I nodded off for a few minutes and missed the show*, Jesse thought reluctantly. *Either that or Clint had shucked off his clothes in record time.*

Clint climbed over him and onto the bed. He reached down and pulled the hand-sewn quilt up from where it was folded at the foot of the bed. He unfolded it and spread it over his partner, covering both of them. "Come here, you," he whispered as he pulled Jesse close. "No sex tonight. You need sleep more than anything else. Let me hold you in my arms and carry you off to dream land."

"Yes, please," Jesse whispered back to him as he lay there weakly.

"I love you, you know," Clint muttered to me as he kissed his ear.

"I know. I love you, too," Jesse whispered back as he struggled to remain awake long enough to say those oh so important words.

"Sleep now, stud," Clint whispered, his words seeming to come from far, far away. "You're safe in my arms until morning. Sleep now, and dream of my love

for you."

Jesse tried to say something, but could not seem to muster up the strength to talk. He just nodded his head once or twice as he felt the dark soft arms of sleep embrace him.

Chapter Three

Jesse walked along the store aisles, staring at the colourful boxes of cereal on the shelves. *Too many* choices, he thought. *Clint is too set in his ways...he always wants the same kind.* He looked up to see Clint smirking at him. "What's so funny?"

"You. Me." Clint hooked his thumb at their surroundings. "Walking around a grocery store like some old married couple."

"We gotta eat."

"I know." Clint's boots clicked on the tiled floor as he turned the corner into the next aisle.

Jesse smiled as he followed. "You were expecting some kind of reaction?" he asked. "Oh my God, the fags are out shopping." He affected a falsetto-like voice and laughed aloud as Clint shook his head. "Maybe this small town isn't so much of a backwater as you think." He tossed a box of cereal into the basket Clint was carrying in his right hand.

"Oh, I think it is." Clint shook his head. "Sooner or later, something bad's gonna happen." It was why he stayed out on his farm so much.

"You could've stayed home like you usually do."

Clint just shook his head. "Can't let you have all the fun."

"Grocery shopping is fun?"

"Well just about every time you come home, you brag about all the hot guys you saw here in town." An elderly grey-haired woman walked past them with a polite nod and holding a grandchild with each hand. "Figured I'd better come along with you...someone's gotta keep you out of trouble."

"I never get into trouble."

Clint snorted.

Jesse just grinned. "We need soup."

Clint nodded. "Next aisle over." He took a few more steps and then his steps slowed. "Now he's got a really nice ass."

Jesse glanced over his shoulder. "Oh yeah." Blue denim stretched tight over the man's butt as he crouched down to read the labels on the bottom shelf. *Dark hair under his hat, rugged good looks. Greek? Maybe Italian.* "Almost as nice as yours."

"Liar."

Jesse dragged his eyes away from the other man and back to Clint. "Don't be like that. You're the guy I want to be with. You're the hottest guy around."

"You're just saying that."

"I mean it."

The clean-shaven man stood up and walked around the corner.

Jesse and Clint exchanged looks and followed him.

"See, I told you there were hot guys in town. Makes the drive in worth it."

"I suppose."

Jesse grinned and gave the other shopper another quick glance. *He does have really nice shoulders. Wonder if he's got a hairy chest?* His red t-shirt fit fairly snug on his torso. *I'd like to take him out in the barn for a little rub-down...* he thought.

"Chicken broth?" Clint asked.

"Huh, oh yeah get some of that." He turned his head.

"You're drooling."

"No, I'm not." Jesse shook his head. *Shit, am I that obvious?* He hoped not. "Christ, can't a guy even take a look without being jumped on?"

"I thought you liked being jumped."

"I was just looking." Jesse protested.

"I know. Just try not to be obvious." Clint kept his voice low. "You don't want to get people offended."

They stepped out onto the street, squinting in the sunlight.

Clint hurried towards his truck. "This should be enough to keep us awhile."

Jesse hefted the box of canned goods into the back of the pickup. "Given your feelings about Nanton, I'm surprised you don't grow enough food to never have to come into town."

"Tried that...can't get coffee to grow."

Jesse laughed. "I'd think you'd enjoy coming to Nanton for the *scenery*."

Clint turned his head. "Not much point in looking."

"There's always a point in looking." Jesse nodded towards a passing cowboy. "Like at him."

"Married, pack of kids."

Jesse laughed again at Clint's tone. "So there's no point in fantasizing?"

"Now I never said that." Clint gave the street a glance, but his eyes did not linger on anyone in particular. "Anything else we need to get?"

"Nope. We already got the whiskey and rum."

"And a couple of two-fours."

"Yep. The essentials."

"So let's head back."

Jesse sighed. "The chores are waiting?" he asked with some resignation.

"There's always chores," Clint agreed. "Remember, you wanted to stay on the farm with me."

"I know." Jesse climbed into the cab. "I know."

* * *

"So tell me about it."

Jesse stared through the window out at the chicken coup. "My first time you mean?"

"Yep, I want to hear all about you." Clint took a long drag on his cigarette. "I don't want us to have any secrets from each other."

"I don't think there's much about me that you still don't know. You've known me for almost a year now."

"Yep."

"I thought you were supposed to quit smoking?"

"You had to quit cause of your lungs. The Doc just suggested that I give these up." Clint gave the cigarette a look and grimaced. "I cut way back on how many I smoke." His brown eyes flicked back to Jesse. "Now quit yer stalling and talk, boy."

Jesse sighed and reached for his drink. "Well, back when I was a teenager, I knew that I was a lot more interested in stallions rather than fillies. I'd know it for years."

"And your folks found out and kicked you out."

"Yep. I ended up in Lethbridge at my aunt's." Jesse tossed back his whiskey and paused while he felt it burn its way down his throat. "I was miserable there, but had no choice. No other place to go. After a month or so, I got a job working at a donut place. Linda wouldn't let me sit around her place all day and I didn't want too. Not with all that religious nonsense she kept trying to push down my throat.

"There were some perks. Free donuts for one, and the chance to check out a lot of fine specimens of manhood as they came and went. The store did a lot of business."

"Get many offers?"

"No, but I know I was being checked out too." Jesse smiled boyishly as he became lost in his memories. "Anyway, one of my coworkers was really hot. Lou was a really nice piece of Italian meat. He was my age too; about six foot three and probably one ninety. Solid build. Hunky. He was a cowboy type, through and through. I had the hots for him the first time I even saw him. But, he was straight and I just accepted the fact that nothing would ever happen between us. Never stopped me from hoping that something would though. I did like spending time with him though and took advantage of every chance."

"Did you spend much time with him?"

"Enough. We hung out after work. Played around at the park—he looked *amazing* in shorts—when we played soccer." Jesse could still picture Lou exactly in his mind. "We were always joking around about sex. He'd say stuff like 'blow me' or 'suck my dick' and I just laughed and said 'only if you promise not to cum in my mouth'. We laughed it off as a joke."

"He didn't know you were gay?"

"No, I don't think so. It certainly was never mentioned around in my aunt's hearing."

"So this one Saturday morning in May, we'd made plans to repaint his old Chevy. We were on our way to the *Canadian Tire* to get the paint and supplies when he suddenly burst out and said 'I promise not to do that in your mouth'.

"I pretended not to know what he was talking about and I asked what he was talking about. He said that he promised not to come in my mouth if I would suck his dick. I told him he was sick and then we just laughed it off."

"But you wanted it?"

"Oh God, did I ever." Jesse took another swallow. "We spent pretty much all day doing bodywork and painting his truck and we started drinking beer later in the afternoon. We drank a lot of beer and after a while, we started joking more. By evening, we'd had enough of that damned truck and were just sitting outside in the dark getting more and more hammered.

"Then Lou said he was so drunk that he would probably suck my dick if I bribed him. So, I told him to go for it. We started bribing each other. I agreed to suck his dick if he would suck mine. But, then he refused to go first and I wouldn't go first either. We decided we needed more beer so we headed over to the ATM to get more money and then we got more beer.

"We drove his truck into the woods behind my aunt's house and sat on the

tailgate of the Chevy drinking. He continued to try to talk me into sucking his dick. I wanted him so bad, but I was afraid it was some kind of joke and I didn't want to ruin our friendship.

"As time passed and it got late, he finally decided he wanted to go home. So, I pretended to lose the truck keys to stall. Later I found them and just before we were getting into the truck to go home, he asked me 'Why don't you go ahead and suck my dick?'

"By then I was afraid it would be my last opportunity so I nodded. 'Okay I'll do it.' He laid back on the tailgate of the truck and pulled his jeans down. He was really beautiful. His dick was at least nine inches long and it curved a bit to the left. I couldn't believe what I was seeing!"

Clint rubbed the crotch of his own jeans. "Sounds really nice." He was obviously getting turned on by the story.

"It was, oh man, it was. Anyway, I was still afraid so I just started stroking it. I mean, I had touched other guys before, but this felt different. Lou was so hard, but it was smooth to the touch. I asked him how it felt as I stroked it and he said 'good'. Then, I asked him 'how does this feel?' as I slowly swallowed his dick. I sucked it and licked the bottom side back up to the head and he couldn't even talk. He could only lay there and moan in pleasure.

"I was so turned on by the way he responded that I grew even more eager to please him. I slowly licked the head and then began bobbing my head up and down while I continued to suck and lick his dick. He had propped himself up on his elbows to watch me while I gave him the best blowjob I knew how.

"Before he came, he offered to trade places and suck my dick for a while, but I was so eager to get him off that I wouldn't stop. I continued sucking and licking and he began thrusting his hips forward. It was difficult not to gag. I just held my head still while he fucked me in the mouth for what seemed like an eternity. Then I started sucking and bobbing my head up and down again until he let out a low moan and started shooting his load in my mouth. I slowly slid his cock in and out of my mouth and continued to lick the head while he shot. He tasted so good. It was a salty, musky taste that I'll never forget."

"And did he return the favour?" Clint asked.

"Nope." Jesse shook his head. "As soon as it was over, he got up and said that he was ready to head back home. He apparently felt guilty and angry and he started backing the truck up really fast and got stuck. So, we ended up spending quite a bit of time in the woods that night."

"Did you stay friends?"

"Yeah, but we never talked about that night and we certainly never fooled around again." Jesse sighed. "I wanted too, but he never did. I couldn't push him into anything so...one day I'll have to go back to Lethbridge and remind him that he still owes me a blow job!"

Clint laughed. "That wasn't your first time though."

"No, guess not." Jesse shrugged. "I got a bit sidetracked."

"All your sexual escapades just blur together?"

"Yeah, I guess that they do."

Chapter Four

Jesse rolled over and stared for a moment at the exposed beams in the ceiling. The moonlight was pouring through the window and Clint had thrown the sheets back. The quilt was tossed down to the foot of the bed, tangled with their feet. *Clint's grandmother had a fine hand for sewing*, he thought as he untangled the quilt. *This must be fifty years old at least.*

Clint was lying face down, but the pillow did nothing to muffle his snores.

And he complains about me *snoring.* Jesse ran his fingers lightly across Clint's back. "No tan lines," he commented softly. "You must be spending a lot of time outdoors naked." He knew that he also lacked the typical *farmer's tan* as well. "You've got a great body for an old guy."

Clint kept snoring.

Jesse's fingers brushed lightly across the mound of Clint's firm ass cheeks. "You've got a great tight ass for an old man," he said softly.

* * *

"Another day done."

"The barn looks good. We're almost done replacing the boards."

"We should be able to start painting it in another day or two."

"I couldn't keep this place up without you," Clint told him.

Jesse smiled. "Keep up the chores?" he asked. "Or something else?" He pressed his hand against the fly of Clint's *Wranglers* and laughed as he groped his lover's crotch. "Seems like something is always popping up around here and needing attention."

"Git away from me."

"You sure?"

"Yeah. Go have your shower," Clint told him.

Jesse headed into the bathroom. He peeled off his sweaty t-shirt and then dropped his jeans onto the tiled floor. He stood in front of the mirror in his tight briefs and checked out his body. The seemingly endless farm work had given him a firm body—hard pecks, chiselled abs, a cute butt, and muscle tone everywhere—and it kept him in shape. *Good thing Clint likes hairy guys,* he thought. *I'd hate to have to shave this off.* He rubbed at the sweat-matted hair on his chest.

He turned on the shower and shrugged off his briefs. He tossed his dirty clothes into the hamper. *Is it my turn or Clint's to do laundry?* He had lost track. When the shower finally reached a warm enough temperature, Jesse stepped in.

While he was washing his hair, the bathroom door opened. Jesse peaked around the shower curtain and saw that it was Clint, dressed in just his white boxers. *Well who else would it be?* he asked himself.

Jesse figured that his partner was going to take a piss or something so he did not assume much of anything. He turned his back to Clint and resumed soaping his chest. Suddenly he heard the shower curtain rattle open and by the time he had turned around, he was standing face-to-face, dick-to-dick, with Clint. The shower cubicle was small, so both of their semi-hard dicks were touching.

Jesse let out a small moan. His cock was getting harder just from touching Clint's dick. He tried to simply stare at his partner, not saying anything.

"Enjoying yourself?" Clint asked as the shower water soaked through his own hair and ran down his chest. His eyes dropped down to rest on Jesse's hard-on. Abruptly, his hands slide along Jesse's back and Jesse could feel his pecks and six-pack press against his own.

Jesse moaned, feeling Clint's warm, hard flesh against his was so stimulating that a little pre-cum started to ooze from his hard cock tip. As he stood there, growing hornier each second, Clint moved his hands up his smooth back. His hands eagerly moved across Jesse's soapy back.

He rubbed his hands in every direction, touching every muscle on his back. Jesse leaned in close and kissed him.

Clint moved his firm hands from his muscular shoulders and slowly dropped them down to his ass. When he had his hands on my ass, he cupped his hands around my ass cheeks and began to squeeze them gently. Jesse's ass muscles tightened in delight. "You've got a really nice tight ass." Clint began to squeeze harder and harder until Jesse was moving his ass forward, thus moving his dick further into Clint's crotch, with each squeeze from Clint.

"I love what you're doing to me." Jesse realized that he was pressing Clint firmly against the wall behind him and tried to stop thrusting forward when he squeezed.

Clint decided to give me a break from the ass message. He slowly moved his hands back up along Jesse's back.

"Let me return the favour." Jesse slipped his arms around Clint's body and began messaging his back. He was extraordinarily strong, and Jesse could feel the muscles in his back as he rubbed them. He was also feeling his torso against the other man while he was giving the message. The feel of his hard muscles pressed against his chest was amazing. They were so close that when Clint took a breath, Jesse could feel his abs flex out and press harder against his own. He could have cum right then, all over him. "Oh God, I'm getting close!" Jesse groaned.

"Glad you're enjoying yourself."

Jesse felt weak in the knees. He could imagine jerking off on Clint's torso, shooting loads of cum on his hairy chest, imagine Clint rubbing the warm sticky cum all over his chest and down across his cock. Jesse's cock leaked even more pre-cum at the thought. He could see Clint holding him like they were doing right there, rubbing their muscular torsos together, with Jesse's cum for lubrication. Jesse was lost in his fantasy, even imagining that the warm, soapy water running down Clint's chest was his hot cum.

He continued to rub Clint's back, then after messaging his shoulders for several minutes, he decided to move down to his ass.

"Oh, fuck yeah," Clint moaned.

Jesse slowly moved his hands down towards his ass. The hot water from the shower head was shooting right at Clint's shoulders so most of the water was running down their chests, but some of the water was rolling over Clint's shoulders and down his back. Jesse took hold of Clint's ass—it was firm, very firm. Jesse had seen it before—how many times now?—and feeling it was ten times better that seeing it.

Jesse began squeezing his Clint's ass. He dragged his eyes back towards his partner's face. His chin was resting on Clint's shoulder and they were ear to ear. When Jesse began squeezing his ass as if he was kneading rough dough, Clint's head cocked back and Jesse saw his face fill with pleasure. He could only see him from the corner of his eye, but he looked like he was going to moan really loud but nothing came out. Then his head went back to its normal position and Jesse lost sight of it. "I'm glad you're enjoying the shower as much as I am." He continued rubbing those ass cheeks.

"We've been doing this for long enough," Clint growled. "Stop all that pussyfooting around."

Jesse realized that they had been messaging each other for ten minutes, at least, and their dicks had been rubbing together for almost that whole time. Their cocks were both rock hard and they were closely lodged together. They were throbbing from all of our action. When Jesse began to pay close attention, he cold feel Clint's cock throb every few seconds in ecstasy. His did too. Their crotches were more or less pressed flat up against each other because Clint was holding on tightly.

Clint moaned as his cock tip touched Jesse's, and then their shafts were sitting

against each other.

Jesse could feel his cock tip lodged against the bottom of Clint's firm stomach. His nipples were as hard as his cock.

So were Clint's.

Jesse leaned closer and slid his chest close enough so that his nipples could rub against Clint's. After playing with their nipples long enough, he decided to make a move instead of blindly following Clint's lead. Jesse tried to free his body from Clint's grip enough so that he could bend down a little.

Jesse slowly bent his knees and slid down Clint's body. He felt his hard cock slip down the shaft of Clint's and lodge itself at the space between the base of his cock and his balls.

Jesse stared at Clint's nipples. He opened his mouth and stuck his tongue out.

Clint looked down and smiled. Then he looked away and started thrusting his dick against him.

"Wow." Clint's erection was positioned almost where Jesse had imagined rubbing his own cock on Clint. The water provided enough lubrication so that Clint's cock easily slipped along the bumpy muscles of his stomach. Jesse looked up and saw that Clint was smiling and his eyes were closed. It looked like he was imagining some intense sexual encounter.

Jesse kept sucking his firm nipples for a while. He circled his tongue around them and then sucked on the entire nipple. Sometimes he flicked them with the tip of his tongue. Clint seemed to like that, given the groaning he was doing.

Jesse dropped further down and took Clint into his mouth.

"Oh God!" Clint cried out and he bucked his hips.

Jesse swallowed as his mouth filled with salty warmth.

Clint gasped for breath.

Jesse stood up. "How was that?"

Clint was leaning against the wall. "Shit, that was amazing," he muttered. "You're gonna wear me out."

"You liked it. That's all that matters."

"What about you?" Clint asked as he reached own to take hold of Jesse's erection. "What can I do for you?"

"I'm fine."

"You sure?"

Jesse nodded. "Yeah."

Chapter Five

"...and so I marched Clint back to the house where his father was waiting for him. His old man was not happy to see either of us. The local fire and brimstone preacher we had at the time had nothing on him when he got his temper up. Eh, Clint?"

Clint was frowning at his neighbour. "Why'd you drag that story up?" he demanded even as the other people around the timeworn harvest table laughed.

"Because it's a good one," Constance Waverly replied primly. Her face was weathered and worn by the passing of years, but it was clear that she had once been a beauty, especially when she smiled. She was wearing a flower-pattern dress that showed more than a few years' wear, but it was still serviceable and looked really broken in and comfortable.

"Your pa was furious with you." Terry chuckled at the memory. He had a thick beard and dark hair. His dark blue shirt strained across his belly—signs that his wife was just too good a cook. "I'm not sure if Morgan was more angry that you'd been stealing apples, or that you'd gotten caught doing it."

Clint shook his head. "Probably both."

Jesse grinned.

"More pie?"

"No, thank you, Mrs Waverly."

"I told you to call me Constance. 'Mrs Waverly' was my mother." She gestured dismissively. "A healthy young buck like yourself should never say no to a second slice of homemade pie." She took his plate away and walked over to the counter to cut another thick wedge. She suited her kitchen—her personality was warm and homey. "More coffee?"

"Yes, please."

"Clint?"

"Yeah, I'd love another cup."

Constance turned towards him and shook her head. "I see that you still haven't picked up any of Jesse's manners." She patted her greying hair back into its bun. "Still, there's hope for you."

Clint snorted.

"You could have done worse for yourself. Jesse's never been anything less than polite to me. Not since he repaid his debt."

Jesse shrugged. "You were very understanding." While hitchhiking, he had stolen clothes from her wash line to wear...and later returned to pay her back for them with his first paycheque from Clint. *Terry's never mentioned anything about the shirt and jeans I* borrowed. He was wearing those very clothes today. *I got dressed and never even thought about it.*

"It's been too long since you left that farm of yours," Terry said. He and his wife shared a knowing look. "You're no hermit."

Constance nodded set a fresh plate of apple pie in front of her husband.

"I like my farm. Always got something that needs doing."

"So do I. But Constance and I find time to socialize. And not just at the annual horse auction. We have *friends*, Clint, and we get together and do things." He shook his head. "When was the last time you did something?"

"We go to Nanton now and then."

"Only when you're forced to go there, Clint. Like when you need to buy groceries or alcohol."

"There's not much else to do in Nanton," Clint protested.

"There's the *Pale Horse*."

"I ain't one for going to the bar."

"There are various street dances. One on New Year's Eve for example. Two or three others in the summer."

"I'm happy staying on my ranch."

Constance shook her head at his tone. "I thought I'd have to send Terrence to hogtie you just to get you to come here for some coffee and pie."

"Nope." Clint shook his head. "You were always the winner of the pie baking competition at the summer fair. Some years, you were the only one who entered. No one else would try to challenge you."

"Yep, I married her for her baking skills," Terry commented.

Constance rolled her eyes. "You hardly visit anymore."

"Jesse and I have been busy."

"Jesse is the reason I wanted you to come over," Constance told him as she finally set a big wedge of pie in front of Jesse. "I was very happy to hear that you had a new worker on that farm of yours."

Jesse had kept fairly quiet during most of the visit. He picked up his fork and stabbed it into the pie. *Still warm*, he thought as the flaky pastry melted in his mouth. *No store-bought frozen pie shells in this kitchen.* The pie was every bit as good as the ones that his mother had baked when he was a kid.

"You need to get away more often. Jesse shouldn't be cooped out alone out there. You need to spend time with your neighbours."

"Maybe they don't want to spend time with me."

Constance chewed at her lip.

Terry snorted loudly. "Because you're fucking Jesse there?" he asked bluntly. "What's that matter to anyone?"

"It does matter," Jesse pointed out.

"It shouldn't."

"You're more understanding than most."

"Pshaw," Constance said dismissively. "I've known Clint since he was a boy...I'm just happy that he finally found himself someone to make him happy."

"Why, Clint, I think you're blushing."

"Shut up, Terry."

Constance laughed. "Don't fret so much. The Lord has allotted us only so much time here on his green earth...there's point in wasting any of it."

Clint settled his white *Stetson* on his head and grunted. "You got the same good view I do."

"It is a good view. I've never been to the Rockies," Terry admitted. "Sometimes I wonder if I missed anything. I've only been to Calgary a handful of times." He scratched his own head under his hat. "Born and bred in a small town with hardly any reason to leave it."

"No worse than Redcliff or Lethbridge," Jesse reminded them over the rustling of the tall grasses in the breeze. "A small town is a small town."

"Nothing wrong with small towns," Clint said. "I don't want to live in no big city. I'm a country boy."

"Me too. Thank God Constance was happy to raise a family here on the family farm."

"I always thought I was a city boy," Jesse told them. "I never dreamed that I was going to end up on a farm. I dreamed about the bustle of Calgary."

"You can have it." Terry spat into the dust. "Too big, too noisy, too busy. Give me the clean air and brilliant stars of the big city anytime."

"You and me both," Clint agreed.

* * *

Jesse lifted his head from the small notebook and looked around the tiny bedroom. It was one of the old bunkrooms used by hired hands back when Clint's father and even his grandfather had owned the farm.

This was my room when I first came here, he thought as he lay on the narrow bed. *This was the room Clint gave me to sleep in, back before we got to know each other.* Before they had fallen in love. *It's not much to look at, but it feels more like home than either of my bedrooms in Redcliff or Lethbridge.*

The room was small, and Jesse had made almost no changes to it since he had moved in. The dark blue, hand-sewn curtains on the window, the rough blankets on the narrow bed were the same simple comforts Clint's grandmother had given to the hired hands. Even the floorboards creaked underneath his boots. Empty clothes pegs lined the wall beside the door and a small window looked out into the fields.

"It's a good place to come and think." Clint had gone to bed, at the other end of the sprawling farmhouse. *I could shout and carry on in here and he'd never hear a thing.*

Jesse turned back to the pages in front of him. They were covered with words scrawled out in blue ink.

"*We talk a lot,*" he read aloud. "*I'm not sure where things are going, but I think he's a great guy. He never says anything profound or does anything superhuman, but he's just a really great guy. He doesn't work me any harder than he does himself. Never asks me to do anything he won't himself. I don't think I've ever heard him say a bad word about anyone.*"

Jesse had written those words last summer. "They're all true too...just as much now as they were back then." He flipped the book towards the end, where there were still some blank pages, and reached for the pen.

Chapter Six

"We should do some painting."

"Painting?"

"Yeah, put some colour on the walls." Jesse gestured to the living room. "Beige is boring."

"Nope." Clint shook his head firmly. "This ain't some whorehouse. I'm not painting it into some frilly girls' room."

Jesse laughed. "So no pastels then?" he asked with a grin.

Clint cursed.

Jesse's smile grew even wider as Clint cycled through an impressive string of curses. "Don't have yourself a heart attack, old man. I don't want to make this place into some lady's parlour. I just want to brighten it up a bit. There's too much white."

"My parents painted this house. They like white and beige. Mom always said that 'white is bright enough for any room.'"

"It's not a colour."

"I like white."

"White is almost as boring as beige."

"So what colour did you have in mid?"

"Pastel mint."

Clint coughed on his coffee.

Jesse grinned.

Clint set his mug down on the table. "Shit. I never know what you're going to say next."

"That's why you love me, right?"

"I guess." Clint shook his head. "Fine, you can paint." He hooked his thumb at the walls. "But it's going to be your job, not mine."

"Fine with me."

"And if I don't like the colours, then you gotta repaint."

Jesse nodded. "Deal." He plopped down into a chair. "I'm game for that deal, Clint. You'll love the new look."

"I'd better."

* * *

Jesse drove into town and drove along the main street. *Clear skies and bright sunshine...a perfect day for travelling.* He pulled up the curb and stopped the truck. The Chevy's engine rattled as it stopped. "Clint really needs to have that thing checked," he grumbled.

O'Connor's Hardware store was small. Jesse pushed open the door and stepped inside. The hardwood floors creaked under his boots. Racks of shelving filled the place. Jesse walked past bins of bolts and nails and screws, past basic tools, towards the back. *A real nice store.* Like most of Nanton, it was obviously still family owned and operated. *No box stores here.* Unlike Calgary.

"Afternoon."

"Afternoon." Jesse nodded to the man who was approaching. *That must be O'Connor himself.*

"What can I help you with today?" O'Connor wore a white shirt, with a dark blue tie, and black jeans. He was in his fifties, with more grey than black in his hair, and had a pair of round glasses perched on his nose.

"I'm thinking about painting the living room of the house."

"Good weather for it. We have a good array right over here." He led the way to wall covered with samples and tins of paint. He leaned against a counter. The paint-stirring machine was there.

"Wow." Jesse stuck his hands into his pockets and stared at the array of paint samples. *Daunting. I'd forgotten there were so many choices. Or at least, I didn't expect O'Connor's to have so many.* It wasn't a big city *Home Depot* after all. *Just some small town hardware store.* "I'm just not sure what colour I want it to be. Anything other than white or beige."

O'Connor nodded. "White and beige are practical choices, but they're not very exciting. Are you looking for something bold?"

"I'd like bold. My partner wants boring."

"I see. Might I suggest something in a pale blue? The colour is nice, yet subtle. Better than white."

Jesse looked at the sample chip the clerk was holding. "Yeah, that's a nice colour." He paused, giving it a second look. "Maybe something a bit darker though." *Clint would hate that colour. I'm afraid that Clint is going to hate whatever colour I choose.*

"This shade perhaps?" O'Connor asked as he picked up another chip from the display.

"Yeah, now that one's perfect."

O'Connor set the chip onto the counter. "How big a room are you planning to paint?"

"Oh, I'm not sure." Jesse shrugged and felt like a fool. *I never thought to measure the damned walls.* "Average size I guess. Twenty by twenty maybe. It shouldn't be much larger than that." His mouth twitched into a smile. "If it is, I'll just have to come back here for more paint."

"Very true. Oil or latex?"

"Oil. Clint said his folks always painted with oil."

O'Connor's eyes narrowed briefly at Clint's name. "Do you have brushes and rollers?"

"No, I don't think so. I'll need some of them as well."

O'Connor gestured to three tins of paint that he lifted from the shelf. "These should be enough for you. If not, you know where to get more."

"That I do." He followed O'Connor to the front of the store and waited while other man rang up the bill. Jesse dug his wallet out of his *Wranglers.* He offered O'Connor his credit card. *All right,* Clint's *credit card,* he amended to himself. *Good thing Clint pays me a wage for working for him or I'd be broke.*

Jesse walked out of the store and towards the parked pick-up truck. "A good job done." He put the tins of paint into the bed of the Chevy along with the paintbrushes, and then climbed into the cab.

Constable Danials drove past, his eyes hidden beyond his sunglasses. He nodded his head politely to Jesse.

Jesse waved back. *Fuck, he's hot. I wish Clint and I could get a shot at him.* He knew that would never happen. Sadly, he put the truck into gear.

* * *

Jesse stood near the kitchen door, staring out into the farmyard. It was still bright for twilight and he could see Clint's nude body as he stood outside smoking. *Okay*, Jesse thought, *technically he's not nude.* He was wearing his cowboy hat, his worn black cowboy boots, and his grey briefs, but he was definitely *au natural* from his ears down to his knees. Clint's body was not very remarkable really. He did not have any tattoos or body jewellery, nor was his body hair shaved off. His body was fit and trim, without any noticeable sagging or softness despite his age. His skin was tanned, showing the long hours he spent working outside. *Okay, he does have a wonderful body.* Jesse liked everything he could see.

Clint turned around as Jesse pushed open the screen door. "Evening." His cock was jutting out to its full seven or so inches, rock hard and ready behind the cotton of his briefs.

"Giving the neighbours a show?"

"Only if they've got binoculars."

Jesse walked closer. The air was cool against his bare torso. "I like what I see."

"Glad to hear it." Clint reached out and ran his hand through Jesse's chest hair. "I like what I see too."

Jesse chuckled. He rubbed his hand along the front of his jeans. "You're getting me all worked up. Parading around like that."

"So we should do something about it." Clint tossed his cigarette away. The bulge in his briefs was getting larger.

Jesse unzipped his jeans and his shucked them off. "Let's do it right here."

"Okay." He reached over and yanked down Jesse's briefs. "Fuck me!"

"If you want it." Jesse stooped down and pulled a condom out of his jeans.

"Prepared for anything I see."

"I always keep a few on me...when I'm around you, I just can't control myself." He slid it over his erection.

"You got lube?"

"Other pocket."

"Shit." Clint shook his head. "You do come prepared."

"Now let's see if we can get you to *cum*." Smiling, Jesse spread a generous amount of lotion over the head and most of the shaft of his cock. Carefully, he placed the head directly on that tight pink circle of a butt hole of Clint's and pressed downward gently.

"Oh..." Clint moaned as he felt the head pressing against his ass.

Jesse pressed down harder and felt, a slight give as the tip started to force its way past that ring of tight muscle. "Relax, Clint, I'll take it easy for you."

"I trust you." Clint groaned. "Oh, it feels kinda good."

Jesse took his time. Clint was tight and he did not want to hurt him. "Be a good little cowboy, and take it like a man!" Jesse barked out suddenly. "You know want to be ridden."

"Oh fuck yeah!" Clint grunted. "Ride me, cowboy!"

Jesse bucked his hips and Clint rocked with him. He felt the heat in his loins and Clint suddenly arched his back and thrust his head up as he cried out. "Oh fucking yeah!" and jets of cum spurted from his cock to splash across the grass.

Jesse cried out as he came as well, feeling his balls pulsate as he pumped his load into the condom.

Clint's cry of unbridled animal passion was deafening as he came for a second time. "Oh my God!" His body shuddered and shook with force of his release. After about fifteen seconds, Clint's body went limp and he started to collapse over the railing. His body was covered with sweat and his skin

was hot to the touch.

Jesse staggered backwards, almost tripping over his discarded jeans. "Oh my God," he gasped. "That was incredible." He looked down at the cum-filled condom hanging from his slowly deflating cock. "God."

"It was amazing." Clint nodded. He had a self-satisfied smirk pasted on his face, as he stood there. He looked as happy as a pig in a mud wallow.

Chapter Seven

The wind whistled almost mournfully as gusts blew across the field, pushing the tall grasses over.

"So much emptiness," Jesse murmured as he stared at the countryside around them.

Clint nodded and gave the reins of his horse a gentle flick. "You should know...you walked across it."

"Well, across some of it."

"Yeah, you told me that hitched rides to get out here?"

"Yeah, I did. I had no car and very little money when I left Lethbridge, so hitchhiking was my only real option."

"Dangerous."

"I know."

"You could've been killed."

"I know, Clint. But I had to travel somehow. I had to get away from there and I didn't have much choice available to me." Jesse shook his head as he thought back to those spring nights.

Jesse trudged across the parking lot. His breath came out as puffs of mist in the cold night air and he kept his hands stuffed into the front pockets of his blue jeans. The early spring weather was still too cool to be outside for long.

He stepped into the heated interior and unzipped his leather jacket. *Ah, warmth*. He walked over to the counter and ordered a coffee from the plump, sour-faced brunette behind the counter. Sipping from the mug, he gave the restaurant a quick once-over.

The usual assortment of truckers. Most of them had *trucker's bellies* with long hair.

Nobody hot, he thought. *No one worth checking out.* Jesse took another drink, savouring the hot liquid. *But hopefully someone will be worth a ride further up the road.*

Jesse finished drinking his coffee and got ready to leave. He zipped up his leather bomber jacket, then stepped back out into the night and let the door close behind him.

Fort Macleod is that way. He looked off to the west, and narrowed his brown eyes as the wind gusted into his face. *When I get there, I can try to figure out how to get to Calgary.* It was a long ways away. *A lot of kilometres still to go.*

There were many trucks parked there, both on the main ramp and in the parking lot further from the road. Looking back down the highway, he saw a new one lumber in. It had to park pretty far back.

After a moment, the driver got out and started toward the men's room. As he got closer, Jesse checked him out.

He was about the same size as Jesse, dressed in a green work shirt and snug faded blue jeans. He had a long blond ponytail, shaggy moustache, and startlingly blue eyes in a deeply tanned face. As he disappeared into the men's room Jesse saw his head whip back toward him for an instant.

"Good." Jesse smiled and stayed right where he was. His eyes stayed locked on entranceway until the trucker reappeared. Sure enough, he was looking to see if Jesse was still here. As he passed by again, his hand dropped to the bulge between his legs and touched it quickly. He did not slacken his pace, but as Jesse gazed after him, he glanced backward again.

Jesse stared at him as he walked all the way back to his truck. As the man climbed back into the bright red cab, he sent yet another look towards Jesse. Then he shut the door.

After a few minutes, the passenger side door opened and he climbed out. He passed in front of his truck, dropped his hand to his crotch again, and lingered a few moments longer before once again disappearing inside.

Jesse strolled over to the big rig. Its windows were darkened so he could not see inside. The engine was idling with a dull rumble. "Gotta take a chance, right?" He reached for the passenger door and pulled it open. He hoisted himself onto the step, and then he was inside. The cab was huge and warm. He could smell leather, diesel fuel, and just a hint of cigarette smoke. Jesse pulled the door closed with a slam, and looked to his left.

The trucker was seated behind the wheel, staring back at him with those incredible blue eyes, wide and frank with lust. His thumb moved steadily back and forth over his basket.

"How's it going?" Jesse asked him.

"Not too bad, but I'm really horny tonight," the man replied in a thick scratchy Southern drawl.

Jesse's grin widened. "Need it taken care of, eh buddy?"

He nodded, then climbed from the seat, and moved past. For the first time, Jesse noticed a curtained partition at the back. The trucker headed through the fabric, snapping on a light, and Jesse followed him into the sleeper. There was a serviceable bed at the back.

Jesse sat on the edge of it. He unzipped his jacket, getting more comfortable. The sound of the zipper was loud in the cab.

The trucker moved closer, unbuttoning his *501's*.

"Allow me." Jesse finished the job and pushed them down his thighs, revealing a decently flat stomach and below, a skimpy pair of blue bikini briefs—a surprise. He put his hands on the trucker's butt and leaned forward until his mouth pressed against the bulge in his underwear. His scent was faint and clean. *So much for the myth of the unwashed trucker.*

The man's breath quickened at the contact.

Jesse reached inside the briefs and pulled the half-hard cock out of blond pubes. It was uncut, but clean. He put it into his mouth and went to work on it. It quickly became rigid and the trucker sighed with pleasure. "Oh man," he whispered. "Oh yeah, suck that cock!"

"Let's get these out of the way." Jesse peeled the briefs down the trucker's thighs to his knees. In a few moments, the trucker was fucking his mouth, slamming his rod into him.

He kept moaning 'Oh man' several more times while Jesse held onto him for dear life, trying to keep his throat relaxed and the spit flowing.

The trucker began to grunt and, reluctantly, Jesse pulled away. "Don't stop," he protested. "I'm so close!" He started to pull furiously at his dick, willing himself to reach the climax so tantalizing near, grabbing at Jesse's head, and keeping him near the action. Small guttural cries rose from his throat as the speed of his hand increased to a blur.

His dick finally spit cum over Jesse's face and tongue in warm spurts. "Oh, man," he cried out one more time.

Jesse swallowed some; the rest dripped onto the front of his green t-shirt and grimy jeans.

"Oh, geez," the trucker said, panting.

"No problem," Jesse replied with a shy smile. "It'll dry."

"Sorry." Abashed, the trucker considerately handed him a roll of paper towels from somewhere nearby and Jesse cleaned himself up as best he could. "You were just what I needed."

Jesse zipped his bomber jacket. "Well, guess I gotta hit the road. Thanks a lot, buddy," he said as he opened the door and clambered out of the cab. He jumped out—the cab higher up than he had expected—and he hit the pavement hard. Breathing fast but otherwise uninjured, he started to saunter across the parking lot.

A police cruiser had stopped nearby. The cop was standing by his open door and glared at him suspiciously, but Jesse simply shrugged at him.

"Hey," the trucker called out, "do you need a lift someplace?"

Jesse turned around. "Where you headed?"

"West."

"Good enough for me." Jesse turned and headed back to the cab. "Name's Jesse."

"Shawn."

"Nice to meet you." He closed the cab door. "Heading up to Calgary by any chance?"

"Nope, but I can take you as far as Fort Macleod."

Well, I could hope anyways. "That's good enough for me." He offered Shawn a friendly smile. "Thanks for the ride. It's a cold night for walking."

"Thanks for the ride you just gave me," Shawn told him. "Maybe we can do that again when we hit town?"

Jesse nodded. "We'll see."

Misty Morning stumbled and broke Jesse's line of thought.

"You okay?"

"Yeah, Clint." Jesse blinked his eyes to clear them and then hastily checked the ground in front of them. "Just a little stumble. Misty is fine." He patted the grey horse's neck.

"We should head back to the house."

"Yeah, I guess so."

Chapter Eight

Clint climbed out of the truck and paced towards the house. He carried a number of envelopes in his hand. "Bills," he muttered as he rifled through them. "Bills and junk mail. Never anything worth reading. Don't know why I bother having a mail box down there."

"Welcome home, stud."

Clint looked up to see a handsome, dark-haired young man staring back at him. All that he had on was a pair of tight white briefs and brown cowboy boots. He was lean and lanky and the perspiration on his hairy chest accentuated his sun-bronzed skin. "Now that is a nice sight to see."

Jesse smiled back. "I've been waiting for you to get back here." He took a step closer. "Care for a drink?"

Clint licked his lips.

"Or maybe we should go for a swim?"

"The pond is probably nice."

"That's good," Jesse replied. "Maybe that's what I need to do. I feel really hot right now." He patted the bulge in his crotch as he looked at Clint. "But first I've got this little exercise routine to do."

As Clint shook his head, Jesse started into a set of sit-ups. "Since when did you start all this?" he asked with surprise.

"Since I want to keep myself in shape."

Clint chuckled. "You work on a farm. That's enough exercise for anyone."

"And it's kept you looking fine." Jesse was barely panting as he began a series of push-ups. "Wonder how it would feel to be underneath me right now?" he asked and Clint shook his head. Jesse knew full well that Clint was watching and so every time he dropped down, he would look over and grind his hips into the grass before lifting back up.

Clint was just standing there, watching, with his hands hooked on his belt buckle.

Jesse finished his exercise routine with some muscle stretches. He stood there in plain tight white cotton briefs with a huge bulge at his crotch. "Go ahead and enjoy the view," he told Clint. He turned towards the farmhouse, giving Clint a wiggle of his butt, before turning the rest of the way around

"Since when did my farm become a nudist camp?" Clint demanded.

"Since I showed up," Jesse replied with a grin. "Though, given the stories you've told me, you were running around here naked long before you found me out in your barn."

"I never should've told you all those stories."

"Yeah, they might come back to haunt you." Jesse picked a plastic bottle off the porch railing and poured its contents over his tanned body. Clear water splashed across his skin, running down his hairy chest and soaking into his briefs.

Clint's attention was riveted on those wet clinging briefs. The water had made them transparent, and he could see the whole outline of Jesse's cock. It was huge, and the shaft bent out in an arc with the thick head tucked under his balls. He shivered in anticipation.

"Watch it grow," Jesse whispered as his cock began to straighten and the head pushed down against the fabric outwards. The wet briefs became so stretched that he briefly wondered if his cock was going to break through them.

Clint could clearly see his slit and the ridge around the swollen head. Before he could reach up to touch it, Jesse pulled his briefs down and his now-freed erection bounced to full size.

"Come here, you." Jesse pulled Clint's t-shirt off and threw it down into the grass. His hands dropped to the front of Clint's blue jeans, fumbling them open.

"You're insatiable!"

"Yeah, maybe I am." Jesse stared at his now-naked partner. "You got any complaints?"

"Nope." Clint's eyes roamed across Jesse's body. "Not a one."

Jesse wiggled his hips and his hard cock bounced. "Want to suck it?"

Clint dropped to his knees in the grass and licked the tip, tasting the salty

pre-cum. He wanted more and opened his mouth wide and closed it over Jesse's thick cock-head.

Jesse moaned and put his hands behind Clint's head and pulled him forward, bending his knees back until his head was in his lap. He felt Clint's hands on his thighs for balance as he continued to lick.

Clint's hands moved down his back to his ass. Cupping his cheeks in his big hands, he squeezed them together and pulled them apart. He ran his forefinger up and down Jesse's crack, playing with the hair there.

"Mmm." Jesse reached for another plastic bottle and poured suntan oil over his cock, lovingly caressing his hard slippery beauty with my hands, while Clint was licking his balls.

Clint rubbed his body against Jesse's, the suntan oil making both men slippery and adding to the sensual experience.

Jesse's legs felt like jello as Clint kissed him. *He always does that to me.* He squeezed Clint's nipples and slipped his tongue into the older man's ear. They were both kissing, running their hands across each other's bodies and generally working themselves into a frenzy. Jesse writhed helplessly and his whole body went into spasms, and he moaned that he was going to come.

With a mighty lunge, Clint thrust his hard cock along Jesse's ass crack and it proved too much for both men.

Clint's grunts and moans became louder and louder and Jesse cried out and sprayed his load across the grass as Clint spent hot spurts splattering across the other man's back

Gasping, Jesse slumped forward and Clint fell forward with him. He kissed Jesse's neck and opened his clenched hands, intertwining their fingers, all the while grinding his hips weakly against Jesse's.

"Shit, that was hot." Jesse's back was soaked with sweat and he felt grit clinging to his chest. "I really need a dunk in that pond now."

"You get me all worked up!" Clint complained as he fell into the grass and lay on his back. "You're gonna wear me out."

"You're wearing *me* out," Jesse protested weakly. "I just wanted a little bit of exercise."

"Right." Clint laughed. "Had enough *exercise*?"

Jesse licked his lips. "For now."

"I thought you were painting the house?"

"I have been. I just needed to take a little break." He stretched his back. "A little breather is good."

"Heavy breather is more like it."

l Chapter Nine

"Did you finish your errands?"

Clint nodded. "Yep. You?"

"Yeah."

"Good."

Jesse shrugged. *What was he doing in the bank for so long?* Surely there was no financial trouble with the ranch. *He'd tell me if there was, wouldn't he?*

"Well, we still got other errands to do." Clint started walking along the sidewalk.

Jesse stood on the street corner. He was staring down the street.

"Who're you looking at?" Clint asked as he turned to look.

"That guy."

"What guy?"

"The one in the red *Neon*."

"What about him?" Clint gave the driver another glance. "He's okay looking I guess."

"He looks so much like a guy I used to know."

"What was his name?

"Phil. Probably wasn't him though." Jesse shrugged as the car drove off. "What would he be doing in Nanton?"

"Passing through most likely." Clint adjusted his white *Stetson*. "Not many people ever stop for long in Nanton."

"I did."

"You were an exception."

Jesse sighed. "I still remember the night that I seduced Phil."

Clint frowned at the name. "He was one of your high school friends?"

"Yep. Not quite as a good a friend as Dave was, but still a close one. We'd gone out this one Friday night to the local watering hole. None of the local women were interested in our any of our sure-fire pickup lines. So, we ended up going home with just each other

"I'd known Phil since kindergarten. We'd grown up together. At the time, he was as straight as they come and I don't think he suspected that his best friend beat off thinking about him. I'd had a crush on Phil ever since I realized I was more turned by men than girls. He had this nice wavy black hair that hung just above his collar, plenty of muscle, and the best chest I'd ever seen. He was trying to grow a moustache too.

"I chased after the local women with him, because I had to. I caught a few, but nothing ever happened. I always ended up feeling bad the next morning, but at least my secret was secure."

Clint snorted.

"I hadn't actually seen Phil naked in the whole time I had known him. I could *imagine* what that bulge in his pants looked like, but I had never seen it. We didn't share the same gym class and there was never a real opportunity to get him naked. Believe me, I'd tried all sorts of things. He was just too shy about his body. This was a source of great speculation and frustration on my part.

"Anyway, getting back to my story, we went to my home with the dreaded *blue-balls*. You know, that disease that single straight men invented to salve their egos for beating off that night. They had to do it because they had Blue Balls, you know the shit."

Clint nodded. "Yep."

"We got to my parents' house—they were gone for the weekend to some out-of-town religious meeting—and that was when I realized that my dear friend had just a little too much to drink that night. I actually had to help him into the door. I got him over to the couch and when he was sitting he seemed to get a little better. "'Those fuckin bitches were teasing us all night long, man,'" he shouted.

"'That's what women do best, you know that.'"

"Right," he slurred. "Fuck 'em.'"

"'That's what you wanted to do anyway,'" I responded.

Phil started laughing at that. "'How about a beer?'" he asked.

"'Sure, but it's getting late.'" It was easily two, possibly even later by then.

"'Naw, still early. Please?'"

I got him the beer out of the refrigerator. It was a running joke that I could not refuse him when he pleaded.

"'Man, it's hot in here.'" Phil proceeded to take off his shirt. He pulled it over his head and tossed it over the back of the couch. This gave me a look at that chiselled chest again, the one with the perfect nipples. His chest is mostly smooth except for the line of black hair from his belly button on into the tops of his jeans. "'That's better.'" He took a big gulp of beer. It was a very warm night, being July.

"'Sorry, the air is broken,'" I apologized, even though I was secretly glad that it was getting hot.

"'No problem, I can always take clothes off.'"

Something in his tone made me look up from the beer I had gotten for myself. Was that some kind of come-on? It was something about the way he said it, something in the tone. I decided to take things very cool and not jump to conclusions.

"'What's on TV?'" he asked.

"'No idea.'" I tossed him the remote. "Find out. I gotta go and take a leak." I heard the TV come on as I left the room.

I almost died when I got back into the room. He was sitting on the couch in his white cotton *Hanes* and watching one of my bisexual videos—a video I kept carefully hidden from my parents. I remembered that I had left it in the VCR from that morning. Fortunately, the scene currently on the screen was a straight one.

"'Hi there.'" Phil smiled at me. "'I didn't know you were into this kind of shit.'"

"'Yeah, well, I don't much talk about stuff like that,'" I stammered.

"'Your parents would freak if they knew.'"

"'Yep. Why don't you turn it off now? I really don't want to see this now.'"

"'Oh, but I do.'" He grabbed that huge bulge in his shorts with his hand and leered at me. "'This bitch is about to get caught fucking this delivery boy. Her husband is about to come in and kick his sorry ass.'"

"'Come on, Phil, I'm already horny. I don't need to see this shit.'" I tried again. The husband *was* about to come in, but he was not going to *kick* the delivery boy's ass—he was going to *fuck* it.

"'Here he comes. Now the shit will hit the fan.'" Phil was really getting into this and there was no way to stop him. I knew, at that point, that our friendship was over. So I figured, what the hell? His bulge had grown to the point where his brief's waistband was pulled away from his body. I could just see the top of his pubic hair from where I was standing. He reached down and rubbed his hard cock one time and then shot me a glance to see if I was paying attention.

"'What the fuck?'" His exclamation made me look at the screen. The husband was forcing the delivery boy down on his knees. He was delivering my favourite line in the whole film: 'What's good enough for my wife, is good enough for me'. I figured Phil was going to get off the couch, slug me, and throw the remote through the TV. Was I ever surprised.

"'Look at this sick shit,'" he said and then looked over at me. "'You like this kind of stuff?'"

I decided to let it all out now. "'Yes,'" I answered weakly. What I did next amazed me probably more than him. I walked over to him. "'You may hate me later, but I have wanted to do this for a long time.'"

Without giving Phil any time to react, I dropped to my knees between his legs. I spread his legs apart and grabbed the band of his briefs and pulled. His huge, swollen cock flopped against his belly, making a slapping sound that drove me wild. His cock was even bigger than I though it was. It was perfect. He had two huge balls hanging under it and I started nibbling on these. I expected to feel him slap me off at any minute but he just groaned as I took one of those heavy balls into my mouth. I began to lick the ball sack and then made my way up to the cock. I ran my tongue around the shaft, just under the ridge. This made him shudder and I felt his fingers in my hair.

"'Ohh,'" he groaned. "'Suck harder.'"

I was amazed now. I had expected that this was going to turn ugly, but instead it had become a full-blown fuck session. I moved up his washboard belly, licking as I went. I made it up to those perfect nipples. I closed in on his left nipple with my teeth. I lightly bit on it and began to suck on it. This seemed to really turn him on. He moaned and that really turned me on. I was pinching his right nipple and sucking on his left nipple when suddenly I felt his strong hands on my shoulders. He pulled my up onto him and pulled my face up to his. We looked each other in the eyes for a full minute. I did not know what to expect. I figured, here it comes: the kiss off. What I got was the kiss-on!

Phil pulled me close to him and I could feel that he was using all of his muscle in this hug. Then he shocked me by kissing me very passionately. Suddenly I knew what I had envied all those women for, his kiss. His tongue shot into my mouth and I thought I would shoot my load then and there. He ran his hands up and down my torso and then yanked the shirt off my back.

I have a very hairy body and this seemed to turn him on. "Stand up and strip for me. Let me see what my best buddy has for me,'" he said thickly. He stroked his cock once and looked at me expectantly.

I stood up and kicked off my shoes and then pulled off my white sweat socks. He reached over and took off my belt, opened my jeans and slid them off me. I was standing there in my red jockey's with a raging hard-on. He ran his fingers through the hairs on my leg and then tenderly slid my shorts off. He looked up at me for a minute and my heart stopped for a second. Was he really going to *suck* my dick?

"'I've never ahh, had a cock in my mouth before,'" was all he said and then he filled his mouth with my rock-hard rod. He sucked it down to the base. I heard my balls slap his chin. His hands closed on my ass and he fucked his own face, using my body. As he thrust my cock into his hot throat and between his eager lips, he gently massaged the cheeks of my ass.

"'Oh shit, I'm cumming,'" I moaned and pulled back in time to blow my load across Phil's face and chest.

Gingerly, he licked his lips and tasted the spunk that was dripping from his moustache.

"'Now it's my turn,'" I said and dropped down between his legs. I gobbled his steel rod like I was starving.

"'I'm going to shoot!'" He groaned and I sucked harder

I would watch him shot later; right now, I wanted to taste his man-juice. True to his word, he filled my throat with his hot jism. His whole body shook as he climaxed. His balls must have been full because his cock pumped until my mouth was full. I swallowed every precious drop and then licked the sensitive cock slit for last drops.

"'Jesus!'" he gasped, "'I have *never* had a blow job like that before.'"

By this time I had collected myself and flopped on the couch next to him. "'So is this the end of our friendship?'" I asked the big question even though I really did not want to hear the answer. This was the most important relationship in my life and I did not want it to end.

Phil looked at me for so long I thought he would drill a hole right through me. It was impossible to tell what was going on inside that beautiful head. Then a grin began to spread across that face and I felt like a lead weight had been lifted from my chest.

"'No, this is just the beginning of a closer friendship,'" he answered with a leer.

It was at that time that I realized that he was not as drunk as he had appeared but moments before. I promptly put that thought on the back burner because he started to massage my cock.

"'Let's go to the bed, buddy,'" he said.

I stood up and took him by the hand. I pulled him off the couch and led him into my room. He flopped down on his back and rested his head on his laced hands. He smiled up at me.

"'Come on down here and get this here little cock hard so that I can fuck you up your firm ass,'" he leered.

Never being one to need much urging, I dropped onto the bed and began to tease his cock head with my tongue. The response was almost instantaneous. His cock grew hard in my mouth in seconds. He turned himself around so that we were in that magic number position, sixty-nine. His mouth felt so hot and inviting on my cock. He pushed me off him, and then pulled up my face so that he was looking into my eyes. "'Can I fuck you?'" he asked. I could see, in his eyes, that he was almost fearful of asking.

"'Yes,'" I answered, "'fuck me, Phil.'"

"'I don't want to hurt you.'"

"'I'll let you know if it's too much.'" I smiled. This brought a smile to his face. I reached into my bed stand and brought out a jar of baby oil.

"'You're sure about this?'"

"'Yes.'" I took the jar of baby oil and opened it. I reached over and rubbed copious amounts of the slick liquid to his hard shaft. He was getting even harder. I got onto my knees and I could feel his head pressing against my ass. "'Shove it in slowly.'"

"Okay.'" He slowly slid his spear home. I felt like my asshole was going to tear open from the size of his prick. "'Feel all right?'"

"'Fuck me!'" I cried out and this sent him into action. He fucked my asshole hard and fast. I could feel the heat radiating from his body in waves. I could feel his sweat dripping onto me. As he fucked, he was rubbing my back and then he slid his hands down and began to caress my hard nipples. I reached down and began to pay a little attention to my own cock. Then I felt his hands reach down and begin to rub my belly. He bent over my back and began to bite on my ear. I exploded right then and there. "'You are the tightest fuck I've ever had,'" he whispered huskily into my ear. Now he slowed his pace way down. He was licking my back and neck, nibbling here and there.

"'I want to watch you shoot.'"

He grunted acknowledgement and continued to spear me. I was hard again by the time he finally pulled out of me. I spun around to see him grab his cock and give it maybe two or three strokes before he exploded over his chest, some of it landing on his chin. He shook from the force of his own orgasm. He pulled me up into his arms and we just lay there quietly. He hugged me to him and then he kissed my lips. I fell asleep like that, in his strong arms.

"So what happened?" Clint asked. He gave himself a shake.

Jesse smiled with the memories. "I woke up to find him standing over me, still dripping from the shower. When he saw me awake he smiled down at me.

"'Get up and get a shower,' he told me. 'Let's do that again.'"

"I laughed at him. 'Phil, I always figured you for a straight guy. I figured last night was just because of the booze.'

"He smiled at me. 'Hell no, I wasn't that drunk last night. I just wanted to be sure of you before I made a move and lost a friend.'

"'Sure of me?'

"'Yeah. I have wanted to make it with a man for a long time. I thought you might be open to a little man to man with me. I've caught you looking at my crotch and ass every chance you get. Especially all those times you seemed to try to catch me nude. I knew you wanted me...and I was willing to try it.'" Jesse took another drink.

Clint shook his head. "So what happened to him?"

"We stayed friends. He was dating some waitress or other when I left Redcliff for Lethbridge, but we still had our *friendly* encounters.

Phil was the guy I was fooling around with in the garage when my dad caught us."

"I thought I recognized the name," Clint said

1 Chapter Ten

"Another cattle auction?" Jesse asked he poured himself a mug of coffee. "This afternoon?"

"Yeah, another auction." Clint leaned back in the kitchen chair and stared across the worn table at his partner. "I'm going to it."

"Checking out the prime beef?"

"Always." Clint chuckled. "Even though I already got me the best bull."

Jesse smiled. "Moo."

A grin worked its way across Clint's face. "You are one silly guy."

"I know."

Clint pulled on his boots. "I'm gonna take Railjumper out for a ride," he said. "Maybe stop down by the road and check for any mail."

"Have fun." Jesse glanced at the dishes in the sink. "I think I'll stick around here and get a few chores done. Get them out of the way before we head into town."

Clint nodded. "You can come with me."

"No thanks." Jesse turned to look at him with a wink and then a leer. "I'll *cum* with you later though."

Clint shook his head.

Jesse walked into the bunkroom and stared at the notebook and pen lying on the bed. He picked it up and flipped through the pages.

Hi Mom, he read his own writing. *I know I don't write you as often as I should but I've been busy and seeing as how tense things were when I left home...well, I just don't think about writing or calling you. I know I should though. I don't want you to worry about me. I've found a job as a farm hand on a farm up towards Calgary. Clint, the owner, works me hard but fair. He's a great guy too...generous and friendly.*

Jesse closed the notebook up. "I really should mail that away." He had the stamped envelop ready too....

* * *

Clint drove his old Chevy pick-up into town just like he drove his horse—hard and fast.

"Just like driving across the prairie in my dreams," Jesse muttered.

"What was that?"

"Nothing."

Even in town, the traffic was light. He pulled up to the curb and the truck lurched to a stop with an awful shudder.

"You ever gonna get yourself a new truck?" Jesse asked as he listened to the motor grind to a stop. He pushed his door open.

"Maybe when this one wears out."

"I think it's already worn out."

"It's fine. It's just got a little character." Clint closed the cab door with a solid thud.

Jesse stretched, and then adjusted his shirt. He was wearing some of his better clothes. *Clint never commented on my snug jeans*, he thought. He had chosen a pair that hugged his legs and butt, without being too tight for public viewing. *Don't want to draw too much attention.* "The auction yard?"

"Yep." Clint was wearing a blue denim shirt and the usual blue jeans. He adjusted his hat and then shook his head at his preening.

"You look fine," Jesse told him.

"Am that obvious?"

"You're just trying to look good."

"I can never look as good as you. You've got youth on your side."

"I think you're hot."

Clint snorted.

The yard was crowded with cowboys.

"Just like every year."

"Always some new faces though."

Jesse looked around. *A lot of nice faces...and nicer butts. Jeans were made for that ass.* This afternoon was going to be torture on him. *So much to see...so much temptation.*

Clint nodded to some of his friends as they walked passed.

Jesse glanced at two young men as they walked past. *Very nice.*

"Good to see you two."

Jesse turned at the voice. "Afternoon, Constance."

She smiled warmly at him. "Afternoon, Jesse. I'm glad to see the two of here in town." She was wearing a knee-length green floral dress and her hair was done up. She had obviously taken time with her appearance, and she looked almost elegant.

"We always come to the auction."

"I've never missed one yet," Clint said. "Not in forty some years. Mom and Dad used to take me. When I was a colt, I used to love coming to town and seeing the animals."

"You hated it as a teenager," Constance pointed out to him. "You raised such a fuss one year that we could hear you down on *our* farm."

Clint snorted.

"I've never missed one the whole time I've been living in Nanton," Jesse pointed out with a grin.

Constance laughed. "Two for two...it's a good record."

"Pardon me." Sam Tennant brushed past, nodding politely to Constance, and pointedly ignoring Jesse.

"I see he's not suffering any." Terry and Clint joined them as the town's bank manager stopped to chat a moment with other businessmen.

"No," Clint agreed sourly, "his stomach is growing faster than a prize sow."

"Where's his shadow?" Jesse asked, twisting his head to look around at the crowds. *So many cowboy hats, so many hot guys.*

"Can't say that I've seen Jonny," Terry said with a frown. "Not today at least."

"I reckon he's around. This is the day to be seen and he never passes up a chance to flaunt himself."

"Speak of the devil and he appears," Constance commented.

Jesse looked.

Jonny was standing next to Sam.

Jesse sighed. *He looks so good.* Jonny was tall and well built, with muscular arms that strained the sleeves of his tan shirt. His jeans were tight against his butt when he turned to watch the first of the cows being led into the yard. *Too bad he's such an asshole.*

Jesse had difficulty keeping his mind on the auction. *Too many things to look at.* Too many hot men. *Where do they hide during the rest of the year?* He wondered. *I never see half of these guys when I come into town.*

"If you gentlemen will excuse me, I see someone I want to speak too."

"I'll catch up with you in a bit," Terry told his wife as she walked away. "Are you two coming to the dance at the *Horse* tonight?"

"Probably not," Clint said.

"We might stop by the *Pale Horse* for a drink or two, but I doubt we'll be joining in any of the dancing."

"Least not with each other." Terry grinned at their startled looks. "Course, Suzie might be looking for you again, Jesse."

Jesse smiled weakly. "I'm sure she's found herself a dance partner for tonight already." At least he hoped so. *She's quite the little wild woman,* he thought. *Enough to tempt me even.*

Clint grunted.

Chapter Eleven

The sudden storm had passed and the low evening sun had broken through the clouds behind him as Jesse slogged along the driveway towards the farmhouse and the barn.

The sound of a truck approaching growled behind him. Jesse turned his head and looked over his shoulder.

The green Ford was pulling a horse-trailer.

Jesse stared at it as the truck drove past him, splashing him as it rolled through a puddle, and then pulled to a stop beside the barn.

A man climbed out of the cab.

Jesse hesitated in going forward to help him because he had already been walking back to unload his horse, but he turned and looked directly at the young man. With the sun behind him like that, all he could really see was his tall, broad-shouldered, cowboy silhouette. He was young though, maybe early twenties, a bit younger than Jesse. His movements were too fluid for an old dude. And judging by the way he stood there and watched Jesse walk towards him, he had a bit of a cocky, arrogant attitude as well.

Jesse frowned. He had been caught out in the weather and felt self-conscious under the other man's scrutiny, his denim jacket and jeans soaked through, and his dark brown hair plastered against his head, a two-day growth of beard on his face. He pulled up the leather-lined collar to catch some of the drips just as a shadow crossed the sun and he could see the other man properly for the first time.

Wow, Jesse thought. *He's got everything that gets me all hot for a guy...and all in one package*—from the fit, muscular body through to the amused blue eyes. It was more than that, though. This person had that unexplainable, irresistible *something*. Jesse gave himself a quick mental shake even as he felt a stirring inside his *Wranglers. Control yourself,* he thought...and realized that he was staring at the serious bulge in other man's jeans. He licked his lips. *Hey! Control yourself.*

You've got Clint...and you don't even know if this guy would be interested in playing around. It wasn't that he didn't think cowboys got it on together—what else would they do, stuck for weeks at a time in all male company—but he didn't fancy an ass-kicking if he guessed wrong. *What would Clint say if I hit on one of his neighbours?*

The man grinned with a flash of even white teeth, his earlier seeming arrogance gone. "So what happened to you? Forget to wear your hat?"

"It blew off." Jesse was not about to admit that he'd chased it for half a mile and still lost it, though.

"Oh." He laughed and, transferring his own hat from hand to head, then proceeded to unload his bay in a clatter and slither of hooves.

"You brought Railrider back," Jesse said. His growing hard-on was tugging at his jeans as he watched the movements of the other man's firm denim-clad ass. But the horse *was* nice and his muscles rippled under its skin as it moved and even though he'd obviously worked it hard that day, it stood proud, breathing in the scent of the other horses on the farm, health gleaming in its burnished coat. A saying from home flashed through his mind. *Fit as fuck—just like its master.*

"So you're Clint's stable-boy?"

"Yep. That's me."

At that moment, Clint stepped out of the farmhouse. He was wearing a blue-checked shirt and loose, faded blue jeans with the right knee ripped out. He glanced at Jesse, then at his stallion, and finally at the other cowboy and a grin spread slowly across his weathered face as he touched his brown hat in greeting. "How you doin', Felix?"

The other cowboy smiled. "Doing just fine, Clint. I was just bringing back your stallion. He did a fine job."

"Good to hear. Hope your mare gets some good foals off him." His brown eyes flicked away from his neighbour and back to his soaked ranch hand. "What the hell happened to you, Jesse?"

"I got caught out in the rain. No big deal."

Clint laughed at him. "I told ya not to head in town until tomorrow."

"We needed to take the truck in."

"And we could've gotten a ride back here if you'd waited 'til tomorrow."

"I got a ride back most of the way." Jesse shrugged. "Too late to argue about it now...it's at the garage."

"All way over in Nanton?" Felix asked.

"Yep."

Felix spat into the grass. "I'll be heading into town on Wednesday. Will your old rust bucket be fixed by then?"

"Sure. Ted'll have my Chevy ready in less than three days. Probably be ready tomorrow."

"Well I ain't going into town tomorrow. I'm going there on Wednesday. You guys want a lift in?"

"If you're going that way," Clint replied with a nod. "That'd be right neighbourly of you."

"Then I'll drop in for you two around tenish. Can you two handle things with him?" Felix asked as he held up Railrider's reins. "The wife's got her folks visiting and she's expecting me back in time for Sunday supper."

"Course we can." Clint allowed Jesse to take the reins and start walking the horse to the barn. "You could've kept him 'til tomorrow ya know."

"I said you'd have him back today and I stand by what I said."

"You're a good man, Felix. Say hi to Rachel for me."

"I'll do that." Felix climbed up into his cab. "See ya around." He started the motor and drove off.

Clint took the reins from Jesse. "Hey, boy," he said as patted the stallion's flanks. "Welcome home."

Jesse shook his head. "Sometimes I think you care about that horse more than you care about me."

"Don't ever joke about that!" Clint said, his head whipping around. "You're the most important thing in my life." He reached towards Jesse with his free hand and pulled him close. "You are the best thing to ever happen to me." He gave Jesse a quick kiss.

"Okay then."

Clint let go and continued towards the barn.

Jesse smiled and followed Clint towards the barn. He lagged behind him as he led the horse to the barn, using the sack of grain Felix had also dropped off as an excuse to be able to watch him move. Jesse felt his cock twitch as he thought about how good it would be to unbutton Clint's shirt and run his hands across his hairy chest. The fantasy continued and Jesse was sucking on his nipples and kissing down his taut belly with his jeans miraculously gone and a pair of chaps in their place.

Clint led Railrider into the warm, dimly lit barn, the dying sunlight catching the motes of dust in its rays, the familiar smells of horse and sweet hay strong in Jesse's nostrils, but somehow everything had changed.

When Clint looked back, he gave Jesse a knowing smile. "You think Felix is hot, don't ya?"

"Was I that obvious?'

"Yeah, you were. Well, to me at least."

Jesse sighed. "Damn."

Clint chuckled. "Felix *is* a cutie. Wife's not a bad-looking gal either. A damn sight better than the old guy he bought that farm from. Now he was ugly...living proof that we evolved from gorillas."

Jesse laughed.

"And his wife." Clint shuddered. "Shit, she had a face longer than Railrider. No kids either."

Jesse brushed his wet hair out of his eyes.

"Where's your hat?"

"It blew away in the storm. I couldn't find it."

Clint shook his head. "Clumsy. Now we'll have to buy you a new hat when we go to Nanton to get the truck."

"Yeah, well shit happens." Jesse gestured to the stallion. "Can I give him a rub down?" he asked as he pulled off his jacket and hung it on a nail. His blue t-shirt was plastered to his chest and back. "Sometimes they get knotted up when they travel."

"Yeah?"

Jesse was acutely aware that Clint was watching him closely as he towelled off his hair, before laying a bed for the horse and forking in some fresh hay. His mouth was dry and his erection throbbed against the restraints of his underwear and jeans. But in the back of his mind, he was wondering if Clint was angry that he was looking at other guys—even harmlessly.

"So what if *I'm* knotted up?" Clint asked. "Know where I can get a rub down?"

Jesse turned around and it was like slow motion. He saw the whitewashed wall, the rope halter hanging on its nail, the bales of straw and the brightly coloured pile of horse blankets, and he saw Clint leaning against the wall beside the halter, the outline of his cock obvious in his *Levi's*. He was hard. And it looked fucking huge.

"Maybe you should take those wet clothes off. You might get a chill." He tossed a blanket on to the bales and sprawled on top of it, his thighs open.

Jesse could not take his eyes off him. *Fuck, he looks so sexy!* Jesse quickly began to strip while his partner watched. He peeled off his t-shirt, then kicked off his boots, and unzipped his jeans, hesitating before he slid the whole lot down, his eyes flickering from Clint's mouth down his body to his groin. And then Jesse was standing there in his white boxer briefs, his jeans round his thighs, and he knew the old cowboy could see the spreading damp patch of pre-cum.

"Show me everything you've got."

The sudden hoarseness in Clint's voice made Jesse push his boxers down. His slim cock caught on the waistband and then sprung free to jut quivering from his body, bigger than it had ever been. He was embarrassed by just how excited he was, by the fact he was making me stand there, his body exposed while he was still dressed.

Clint took his time watching and studying Jesse's body.

Jesse licked his lips as Clint finally reached for his own fly. He stroked the bulge there for a few moments, and then slowly teased the zipper down, inch by inch. Jesse stood mesmerized, his arms loose at his sides and his cock trembling as his breathing quickened.

Clint laughed as he zipped back up and got up from the bales in one athletic movement.

Jesse's heart thumped and he closed his eyes.

He heard Clint step across the floor towards him.

Jesse kept his eyes closed as he felt Clint's tongue dart out and lick him. His lips closed on his earlobe. Jesse was aching for him, his engorged prick straining and slippery with pre-cum.

"I'm going to fuck you," Clint whispered in Jesse's ear.

Jesse groaned and his hands moved to stroke his chest and tight tummy, but he did not touch his twitching cock.

Clint pulled him against his body and Jesse felt the heat and hardness of Clint's denim-trapped dick against his naked ass, and the denim of his jeans rubbing against the flesh of his thighs.

Jesse still had not opened his eyes, still had not moved. Jesse felt two fingers on his mouth and his lips parted, catching them. He sucked eagerly, curling his tongue around them, tasting his skin. Clint's mouth left his ear and began to work its slow way round to his throat, leaving a wet trail of saliva. His breath felt as if it were almost burning his skin where it touched. He was in front of me now and his left hand was caressing his shoulders and back, stroking over the swell of his buttocks.

"Stay still. Keep your eyes closed."

"Whatever you say." Jesse groaned again as Clint parted his cheeks with his fingers and his anus clenched involuntarily as he touched it. Clint's fingers pulled out of his mouth and dropped to his chest, his wet fingers leaving trails across his warm skin. He found an erect nipple and pinched it. He gasped and he brought his mouth close, sucking it while his tongue slid up underneath. And all the while the fingers of his left hand were stroking up and down Jesse's crack, caressing against his tight rosebud, slipping inside.

Clint's tongue entered his mouth, filling and exploring and he sucked and kissed back, feeling the graze of new stubble against his skin. Clint's index finger probed inside, sliding in and out of Jesse's hot, excited hole. "Oh yeah," he moaned as his left nipple was trapped between the other man's finger and thumb, being exquisitely twisted and turned and squeezed and pulled, and then it was his right nipple.

"Keep your eyes closed." Clint's hands withdrew and it was murder to obey.

Jesse stood and waited and for a moment, nothing seemed to be happening, then he heard the swish of clothes and the rasp of zippers being undone. And then Clint's hand was guiding his head downwards. Jesse knew that Clint's chest was naked a split second before he pressed his left nipple against his mouth. Jesse's tongue grazed the nipple as he sucked while an unprecedented surge of desire coursed through him and threatened to make his aching prick explode. Finally Clint's fist closed round Jesse's throbbing shaft, squeezing viciously, and Jesse moaned around his nipple and sucked harder drawing it deeply into his mouth, his tongue flicking and pulling the nipple, his teeth nipping.

Clint pulled back and Jesse felt his strong hands on his shoulders pushing him down. His legs did not have the strength to defy the other man even if he had wanted to.

Jesse could felt a white bolt of pleasure hit his loins. He could smell the hot, raw smell of Clint's hard cock before he began rubbing the slick, velvet-soft head over his face, his eyelids, and his mouth.

Jesse knew he was watching as his tongue flickered over and over the glistening dome and probed inside his piss slit, tasting the sweet, salty pre-cum.

Clint caressed the nape of his neck as he licked under the flange and he guided his prick into his mouth. Jesse sucked at the shaft, his hands reaching up automatically to stroke the shaft and fondle his full balls.

Jesse groaned as Clint's rigid prick slid over his tongue and finally Jesse opened his eyes and met his blue gaze.

Tenderly, Clint touched his lover's cheek and stroked his shoulders as the younger man tried to relax his throat. Clint's big demanding cock filled his mouth and pushed, and then it was sliding down the smooth walls of his throat. Jesse's own erection kicked back to life as Clint fucked his face, his hips thrusting as Jesse hummed to make his throat vibrate. Clint's head drew back and Jesse ran his eyes over his lover's tanned, muscular chest, taking in the shadow pattern of hair, the erect nipples glistening with his saliva.

He pulled away, gasping, and jerked me to his feet. Jesse kicked off his jeans and underwear and Clint pushed him in the direction of the bales of straw. Jesse turned to look back at him and could not take his eyes off Clint's huge dick.

Clint did not give him a chance to think, but pushed Jesse onto the blanket, and tugged his knees up and open, placing his bare feet against the scratchy straw bales to hold the position. Jesse's naked body—hard cock and his smooth, tight balls, and all—were all exposed to Clint as he reached for his discarded jeans. He ripped the condom packet with his teeth and pushed two spit slick fingers into his hole as he unfurled it over his raging dick. He squirted gel straight onto the head of his prick and Jesse bit his bottom lip as Clint's fingers withdrew and he pressed his hot slippery cock against his hole.

"Relax. I'll only do this if you really want it."

"I do."

"Certain?"

"Yes. Fuck me, Clint!" Jesse gasped and cried out as Clint thrust himself forward.

Clint's fingers closed round Jesse's hard dick and the ranch hand was sweating and panting, straining to open for him as he pushed in steadily. His head was thrown back and his eyes were closed as he felt his big cock fill his tight little hole.

Jesse grunted as he spurted pre-cum. He felt the soft sweaty mangle of Clint's pubic hair grind against him, soft balls against his ass cheeks, his hard, thick prick throbbing inside him. Clint's fingers slipped up and down Jesse's shaft and his thumb smeared pre-cum all over the head, as his hips drew back and he began to fuck with more vigour. Jesse found his rhythm and bucked back against him, matching his thrusting cock, squeezing it with his ass muscles, while he was jacked off in return.

Jesse cried out, his balls clenching.

And Clint pulled out and flipped Jesse over onto his knees against the bales, his raw hard-on plunging back inside, his hand jerking his cock.

"Oh Christ. Oh fuck…" Jesse tried to hold on while Clint bucked back against him.

Jesse felt the orgasm rip down from his throat and tear down his belly into his balls. Clint shoved himself back inside Jesse even as the younger man was screaming with orgasmic pleasure and shuddering and spurting onto the golden straw, his ass muscles clamping down on his pounding prick, throbbing, milking him.

Clint groaned as his hot cock kicked deep inside Jesse and shot his load, which was still coming, covering his hand with his sperm. He collapsed down onto his back breathing hard, and then Jesse turned his head and kissed Clint, his tongue in his mouth as his cock slipped out.

"Fuck, that was amazing." Clint smoothed back his sweaty hair and grinned. "You gotta go into town more often."

Jesse shook his head.

Chapter Twelve

Seated in the bed of the green Ford pick up, Jesse read the *Welcome to Nanton* road sign as Felix roared past it. The sign still read 'Population 1500'. *Shouldn't it be 1501?* Jesse wondered. *Small town Alberta, I never thought it would be the place I'd want to live. I always dreamed about Calgary or the oil fields.* He grinned as he considered how things had turned out. *And yet here I am.*

Felix pulled up to the side of the road outside the main stores, and turned off the engine. "Here you go, guys."

Jesse climbed over the side of the bed and dropped to the sidewalk. "It's still not much of a town," he commented. He stretched out the muscles in his back, and then hitched up his jeans.

Clint grinned as he closed the cab door. "Yeah, it's not much, but it's the closet thing we got. I sure as hell ain't running all the way to Calgary to buy my groceries."

"Fort MacLeod is a hell of a lot closer than Calgary," Felix pointed out.

"True," Clint nodded. "But it's still too far away. We got a liquor store, a *Tim Horton's*, a drugstore, *O'Connor's Hardware*, a post office, the *Pale Horse Saloon*, what else do you need?"

Jesse shook his head. "I need a new *Stetson*."

"So it's off to *Stedman's* then."

"I guess so."

"Thanks for the lift, Felix."

"You're welcome, Clint. Anytime." Felix drove off with a squeal of tires.

Clint and Jesse stepped through the door into the air-conditioned interior.

"This would look good on you."

Jesse took the black hat. "You think I need a black one?"

"You would look good in black."

Jesse tried it on his head and looked in the mirror. "You like?" It did look good on him. *I've got the colouring for a dark hat.*

"Yeah. It looks good on you."

Jesse glanced around the store. "Now he looks good."

Clint looked towards the man standing near the shirt display. "Too skinny."

"He reminds me of Phil." Jesse put the hat back on its stand. "I don't know if I see one I really like all that much."

Clint shrugged. "Lots of good hats here."

Jesse glanced around the store again. "Wow!" he exclaimed.

"*Wow* what?"

"Over by the pants."

Clint turned his head and looked at the sales clerk. "Is that the type of guy you prefer?" he asked in a soft voice.

"You're the kind of guy I want," Jesse replied instantly, "but he *is* the type I like to fantasize over." The sales clerk was a real cock shocker. He was tall and blonde with that fresh scrubbed look of a college type just between man and boy. Jesse stared into his hazel eyes and the sales clerk returned his gaze, but with the tip of his tongue licking his lips.

"Hello?" Clint interrupted. "Remember me?"

"How could I ever forget you?" Jesse asked innocently. "You're the guy I want to be with." He drifted towards the jeans display.

Swearing under his breath, Clint followed.

"How about some new jeans?" As they searched through the pants on display, Jesse's hand touched Clint's hand and tentatively gave it a gentle stroke.

Clint looked startled, but gave him a look of approval and then he squeezed his hand affectionately. As distracted as Clint was, he finally found some black jeans in what he thought should be his size. "I should go and try these on."

Jesse nodded. "Sure, you do that."

Clint walked towards the fitting room.

Jesse watched him. *He has such a nice ass in those jeans.* "You should try wearing a pair that's a bit more snug. Shows off your assets better."

Clint turned his head and glared back over his shoulder. "Keep it down!" he growled. "We're in public."

Jesse shrugged. "Don't be so shy," he replied. The store's other customers had vanished and they were the only ones in the area. By the time he reached the little booth, he already had the beginnings of an erection bulging the front of his jeans. Clint was so sexy to watch that he could hardly stand it sometimes.

Clint stepped into the room and pulled the door closed.

Jesse looked around with a bored look on his face. No one else around, not even the sales clerk.

As Clint pulled off his pants, he suddenly became aware of something

strange. He looked down and saw two hands wrapped around his waist and fondling the bulge in his briefs. "What the fuck?"

"You were daydreaming." And while he had been daydreaming, Jesse had slipped into the cubicle. He stood behind Clint, resting his chin on his shoulder, and grinding his denim-clad groin into the other man's ass, while his hands worked on his partner's swelling cock. "I hope you don't mind," he said in a sexy whisper.

"Shit!"

"Keep it quiet...we don't want the whole town to hear."

"Get out of here."

"Why? Afraid that you might lose control of yourself?" Jesse kept stroking the growing bulge.

"You're gonna get us thrown out." Clint shook his head. "Christ, you're gonna get us arrested."

"Maybe Constable Danials will frisk us." Without another word, Jesse stepped around Clint and dropped to his knees, then pulled his *Hanes* briefs down and unfolded his sweaty, swelling hard-on. Without a sound, he licked it several times with his warm tongue, then slipped it into his mouth, making it tingle and swell. As he sucked, his hands reached around his lover and clutched both of his butt cheeks. His strong young hands massaged those muscular globes.

Clint grunted. "Hot damn!" he swore. "Jesse, you're—"

A door opened. They both froze and turned, but it was only the door of the next booth. Someone was using the next stall, standing only half a metre away.

Jesse was still for several seconds, but then his tongue started moving slowly over Clint's hard-on again. It had started shrinking when they were interrupted, but now it surged deep inside his mouth again, making him moan slightly. His own hard-on was bulging inside his *Levi's* as he reached up and unbuttoned Clint's pale green shirt.

Clint pulled him to his feet. "I love you," he mouthed.

Jesse smiled and pressed himself against Clint's body. He felt Clint's erect nipples pressing through his thin t-shirt. He dropped a hand to his own jeans, yanking the zipper down and allowing his own cock to spring forth.

Clint hugged him tight, pressing his stomach against Jesse's and mashing their hard cocks against each other.

Jesse opened his mouth and his tongue swirled like a tornado over Clint's tongue and teeth. It became a duel of lusting tongues as they kissed deeply as only two men can.

The person in the next stall was still busy changing clothes and did not seem to be aware of what was happening on the other side of the thin wall.

Jesse was grinding his cock against Clint's and he could sense he was about to explode. "Shit," he whispered, but he could not slow down and with a contorted look on his face, jets of white cum shot all over their bellies and ran down to his still hard cock.

He gave Clint a sheepish grin. "Whoops."

Clint smiled as Jesse tried to wipe cum from the front of his t-shirt. "You done?" he asked as he studied Jesse's face.

"Not quite." Jesse dropped back to his knees. He took Clint into his mouth and began to suck softly

Clint gasped, mindful of the occupant next door. His hand stifled the noises

coming from his mouth as he started to buck his hips.

The unsuspecting soul in the next stall was slipping out of some clothing, hanging it on the wall hook, but still did not seem to suspect anything unusual.

Suddenly, Clint let out an involuntary little gasp of air. He put his hand

back over his mouth quickly and listened. The person next door was just opening the door and leaving. He resumed rocking in and out of Jesse's mouth. "Fuck!" he gasped as he came.

Jesse swallowed as fast as he could.

They drew apart and tried to catch their breath.

"Fuck, that was incredible." Clint shook his head. "You're crazy!" He began to button up his shirt.

Jesse used a tissue from his jeans pocket to wipe his chin clean. "I needed that." He looked at the front of his t-shirt. *Not too noticeable,* he thought. *I hope.*

Clint tucked his shirt back into his jeans. "You *are* crazy," he repeated.

"You loved it." Jesse smiled. "So did I." He opened the door a crack and peeked into the store. "No one's there."

"Thank Christ." Clint hurried back out, carrying his new jeans.

Jesse followed him.

1 Chapter Thirteen

The sun was beating down. Jesse and Clint were working hard, pulling weeds and picking stragglers out of the vegetable garden.

"We should stop by the pond later and cool down."

"It's hard to cool down when you're around."

Jesse laughed and shook his head. "You're a fine one to talk, Clint." You get me all worked up."

"You just like having sex in that pond...you jump me damn near every time we go swimming."

Jesse shrugged. "I've always like water."

"Oh?"

"Yeah...." He nodded. "There was this one time when I was out on Jim's farm for the weekend—one of my high school buddies and he lived just outside of Redcliff—and we'd been tapped to go out and do some weeding in the fields. His folks were away in town for the day and had left us alone. We'd just finished a large portion of the field when we came upon a pond I didn't know they had. I asked him if it was a cow pond, and he made my day when he told me it was a swimming hole. I guess they had built it the year before as a kind of outdoor pool. It was well fenced off—to keep the cows out of it—and as we got into the fenced area, I notice the beauty of it. The floor of the pond was sand—and somehow they had a filtering system set up as the water was fairly clean. There was a grassy area on one side with chairs and a couple of fountains that shot water across the pond. I wanted more than anything to take a swim in the pond. It looked great, and we were both hot from the long day in the field. I asked Jim if we could swim in it, and he said 'Course we can. We'll just have to go back to the house to get some trunks.' I took a chance, and suggested we just go in our underwear."

Clint smiled. "And what was his response to that?"

Jesse returned Clint's leering smile with a matching one. "He said that that he was ok with it if I was."

"And you certainly were."

"Damn right I was.

"He pulled off his t-shirt and started undoing his belt buckle. I turned my back to him when I was taking my jeans off. Not out of any sense of modesty of course, but to hide the huge erection I was sporting. Jim was a hot guy and this was the culmination of a fantasy come true.

"When I turned around to get in the pond, I saw Jim jump in completely naked! I stood there in awe for a second, then figured I best get in the water before he saw my rod sticking through my boxers.

"The water was awesome. Perfectly warmed by the sun, and perfectly

occupied by my now-naked friend. We swam around for a bit and shot the shit. I asked about his plans for college, and he asked me all the usual junk about college—classes, grades—and how many girls I had slept with etc.

"Then he suggested we play a little water wrestling. Now I was in a bind.

If I said no, he would wonder why; if I said yes, he would almost surely find my hard-on. So, I took my chances—after all, this way I could *accidentally* run his hand across his cock a couple times I figured."

Clint nodded. "Good thinking."

"So, we took position in the centre of the pond. The water was about two meters deep, and the sand floor added an extra obstacle to the game. Jim climbed out of the water—God, it was so hot seeing him splash ashore with water streaming down off his muscular back and legs—and flipped a coin in the air to see who would take position behind who. He won, which bought me a few more seconds before being discovered. Watching him leave the pond had gotten me all hard again.

"Jim got behind me and put his muscular hands on my shoulder and side. We counted to three—and at two and a half, I was under the water wondering what hit me.

"I found his feet and yanked them out of the sand, using the little footing

I had as leverage, and soon he was underwater with me. He fought to regain control while I fought to break free. As I pulled away, he grabbed my underwear and literally ripped them off. As we came to the surface and gasped for air, he threw my now-useless boxer shorts onto shore with a laugh. 'Now we're completely equal.'

"With that said, he swam over and, instead of grabbing me to throw me under again, he grabbed the back of his neck, pulled his face to his and stuck his tongue into my throat."

"No fucking way!" Clint exclaimed.

"Yeah. I was in shock. I didn't know what to do—the object of my secret lust for so many years was now kissing me like I had never dreamed possible!

"I was brought back to reality—or heaven—when I felt his hand stroke my

cock. We kissed hard for a long time, until I broke the kiss and guided him by his cock to the shore. When we got out of the water, I almost died. His throbbing cock was at least nine inches long. His shaved balls hung well below, and he was the perfect thickness. I instantly dropped to his knees and took his nuts in his mouth. His balls were huge, and very smooth. I sucked his nuts hard for a while, and then moved up to his pole of manhood. I took the head in his mouth, and licked the pre-cum from the tip. I couldn't wait any longer, and I guess Jim was ready too, because just as I went to swallow his shaft both of his strong hands grabbed his head and pulled me down. I choked a little at first, but was soon accustomed to the cock that was fiercely fucking my mouth.

"I could tell that Jim liked having his cock sucked, and I wanted to show him how much I liked doing it. I grabbed his ass cheeks and took over for him—forcing me to fuck his pole with his throat. I even worked a finger up his ass, and

played around for a while, then I felt him reach around and stick one of his own fingers in past mine. I took that as a hint, and forced two more fingers in his hole.

"He grabbed the back of my neck and forced my head all the way down and

would not let go. I felt his hot ass cheeks clamp on my fingers, and I knew I was going to get the cum bath I had dreamed about. He shot load after of his hot teen spunk in my throat, and I swallowed all I could.

"After what seemed to be a good solid minute of cumming, he pulled my head off his cock, and pulled me up into a hot kiss. We sucked each other's tongues and he sent me into yet another level of shock when he stuck his tongue in his ear and whispered 'I want you to fuck me, Jesse.'

"I wasn't about to question him as his cock was screaming for a release. He turned around and exposed his hole. He had two fingers working things out—so I spit-slicked his cock, and went to enter him.

My cock slipped into his hole easier than I had expected, and I knew he was not so new at this. I did wonder for a moment about who else he might have been with—we had a lot of hot friends I fantasized about—but was brought back to the events on hand when he slammed his hot ass back on my cock. I could tell right away he wanted it rough, so I spanked his ass hard and started pounding my cock deep into his ass. I fucked him hard, and kept slapping his thighs to add to the fun.

"Christ, I was ready to cum well before we got in the pond, so it didn't take long for me to shoot my spunk in his ass. He turned around, sucked my cock clean, and then came up to kiss me again. We kissed for a while and then decided to head back to the house, carrying our clothes while we dried off."

Clint whistled. "You do get around, don't you?"

"I was young and foolish." Jesse shrugged. "I don't regret anything I did when I was younger."

"You never should."

1 Chapter Fourteen

Jesse lay on his side of the bed. Moonlight was shining through the open window and the night breeze played across his bare chest.

Clint rolled over and opened his eyes. "Still awake?" he asked softly.

"Yep. Just thinking."

"What'cha thinking about?"

"My misspent youth."

"Oh?"

Jesse nodded and closed his eyes. He yawned.

"Think about the errands you have to take care of tomorrow."

"I know." Jesse did not bother to open his eyes. "I've got to run to the store and lay in the provisions we need for the month."

"And the extras."

"Yes, and get all the extras."

"This little party was your idea." Clint rolled over and put his arm around Jesse's shoulders.

"I know." Jesse fell asleep.

Lying naked on top of the bed sheets, Jesse's cock rested lazily on top of his right thigh. *I can feel every minute of the work we did today,* he thought. The dull ache of his muscles slowly crept through his body as he lay there, relaxing. *An honest day's work at least.*

Jesse began to slowly stir as he felt the touch of somebody's lip pressing against his. His eyes began to open.

"No, don't open them. Keep your eyes closed," a voice whispered in his ear.

What game is Clint up too? Jesse was growing ever more distracted by the feelings and sensations spreading throughout his body. *I hope it's Clint.* The lips continued to press against his, a tongue gently licking each lip before gently pressing to part them. Pressing, but at the same time teasing, parting the lips but never pushing into his mouth, his mind screaming to feel the intruding tongue caress his, but to no avail. Jesse pushed his tongue forward hoping to force the issue but it only resulted in the lips breaking off entirely.

Moments passed, the breathing heavy can be heard, the sense of anticipation becoming more expectant. When and where will the next touch come from? *How long will I have to wait*? Mind racing. Heart pounding. Then the wait is over, but more confusion filled him. A hand or fingers brushed gently over his face, making his nerves tingle. But there was something else, another sensation rippling through his body. Some feather-like touches are passing over his feet. At first, he couldn't tell what was touching them, but soon it became clear—lips and tongue caressing the toughened skin.

"Mmm," Jesse moaned. *There must be more than one person here. There must be.*

Subconsciously, Jesse's head moved from side to side as the sensations continue to take over his entire being. Again Clint's lips pressed against his gently at first, then with more passion. Soon he feel his tongue being enveloped by the one invading his mouth, could feel the hands that were caressing his face have now slowly moved down to his neck and shoulders.

A shiver racked him. Jesse realized that a cold breeze was passing over them. Normally that wouldn't bother him, but he slowly he realized that his toes were wet.

Since when did Clint develop a foot fetish? he wondered briefly.

Even as Jesse tried to take stock of his situation, he became aware that his cock, which had been resting lazily, was now standing very firmly to attention. The sensations grew with intensity with every new feeling running over his skin. The hand once on his shoulder was now caressing his chest. His body jolting as fingers tweaked each nipple gently at first then growing in strength. The touches on his feet were now slowly moving up his legs. A cool wet trail of saliva created in the wake. Anticipation of the first touch of his hard cock grew and grew. But whomever it was doing these things knew how to tease and draw out the proceedings.

"Oh, fuck yeah," Jesse moaned. "Oh, Clint...." Every last nerve in his body was a raging fire of passion, always wanting to open his eyes to see his tormentor. But with any sign of movement from his eyes his tormentor told him to keep them closed.

Then something changed; something happened that almost pushed him completely over the edge.

He felt a tongue touch the base of his cock, simultaneously, as the feeling of something pushing against his mouth. Something that was wet against his lips. Slowly, he opened his mouth and instantly it was filled with a semi-hard cock, which began to harden the moment it entered his mouth. The taste of precum filled his taste buds, he raised his head to take more of that man-meat into his mouth. The moment Jesse filled his mouth completely with the delicious tasting cock, he felt the head of his own cock be enveloped by something warm and moist. His legs were pushed open by smooth skinned hands and they parted willingly, welcoming any touch or feeling that may arrive in time.

"Mmmm." The cock filling his mouth slowly starts to move with a steady rhythm, a rhythm that is matched perfectly on his own erect cock. He could hear groans coming from somewhere. *They sound familiar.* Then, as suddenly as everything has happened, it stopped.

Apart from one final thing—a realization that his stomach and chest was wet.

"Christ." Slowly Jesse started to open his eyes. This time there was no voice telling him to keep them closed. He lifted his head and looked around.

The bedroom had grown darker as the moon had moved behind a cloud.

Clint was snoring loudly.

Jesse looked at him and blinked once. "Was that just a dream then?"

The breeze played lightly across his naked body and he shivered. He looked down and saw that his stomach and chest were covered in cum. Even as he watched, his cock is on its final decent, the last remnants of cum seeping from the exposed head. It appeared that the juices that covered him were his own.

"What a dream." He let his head drop back on his pillow with a groan. *No wonder I'm so tired all the time.*

* * *

Jesse put the last of the cartons into the Chevy's cab and closed the door. He looked at the drug store and its sign for the post office. *I really should go in there and mail those letters off,* he thought to himself. *I've got four or five of them now. Canada Post* had an office right there. It would only take him a minute. *Would my folks even read a letter from me?*

Time was passing quickly. *For all that he dislikes Nanton, Clint sure keeps sending me into town often enough.* It seemed like he was there every other week any more. *Course, once winter sets in we hardly leave the farm.* He did not relish another snowbound winter.

He eyed *The Pale Horse Saloon* across the street. "Stopping in for one drink won't hurt, I guess." Clint would be expecting him home, but what was the rush? "One drink." He walked across the street and stepped through the doors.

Not surprisingly, the bar was fairly empty.

"What'll you have?"

"Draft beer." Jesse took the mug from the bartender and wandered over to a table. He had his pick—almost every one was empty. *Everyone must at work.* He sat down and took a drink. *This place is usually packed at night…how does the bartender earn his own pay during the day?* He took another drink.

"Well look what we have here," a voice slurred.

Jesse looked up. "Shit," he mumbled.

"This ain't no queer-bar, boy." Jonny glared down at the other man. "We serve men here, not sissy drinks with paper umbrellas."

"Do you see a paper umbrella in my beer?" Jesse asked him coldly.

"Why don't you take your drink and go somewhere else with it."

"Why don't you just leave me alone."

Jonny plopped down onto one of the empty chairs. His black t-shirt was stretched tight across his torso, tight enough to show his abs and pecks. He was a man who worked out and wanted everyone else to know it. "This town doesn't like your kind, sissy-boy."

Jesse said nothing.

"You got no right to come here into town and tease our women," Jonny continued. "You don't even like women."

Jesse shook his head. "Are you still ticked off about Suzie?" he asked. "Christ, that was last summer. We just danced. Nothing more than that."

Jonny's face was turning red.

"You were off drinking with your buddies and she was lonely so she asked me to dance with her." Jesse gestured to the dance floor. "You should be happy she chose me…a guy she can dance with and who is not the least bit interested in stealing her away from you."

Jonny snorted. "You stay away from her," he growled. "Or else."

Jesse looked back at him.

Jonny stood up. "You hear me?" He turned and stumbled to another table where two of his buddies were slumped.

Jesse calmly took another drink of his beer. "I'm not being chased out of here," he told himself. "I have as much right to be here as they do." No one else was taking any notice of him. *Look at him over there, flaunting his body and then taking offence when he gets noticed. If I made a pass at him, he'd deck me.* His buddies weren't bad either. *Mitch is on the skinny side, but has a nice face and Dave was husky. I bet they'd look hot, getting it on.*

Jesse finished his beer and stood up. He walked out of the bar.

Chapter Fifteen

The sun was low in the sky, the light spilling over the crest of the Rockies.

"Isn't that just the most spectacular sunset, Jesse?"

"Yeah, it's nice. More wine, Constance?"

"Yes please. We're just having too much fun," Constance exclaimed. She was grinning widely as a sudden gust of breeze tugged at her skirt. Her blouse was half-undone, showing a hint of cleavage. "And you've finally listened to me. 'Mrs Waverly' was my mother-in-law."

"Got it." Jesse refilled her wine glass. "Glad that you all could make it."

"I don't recall the last time that Clint hosted a barbeque." Terry was swaying on his feet. "Years and years it seems." He adjusted his *Stetson*.

Constance nodded. "Oh, it's been a decade at least."

"Surely it ain't been that long." Clint kicked at a clod of dirt with his boot. "I've never been big on entertaining."

"You were Nanton's resident hermit."

The bonfire crackled.

Constance waved her hand at the farm. "Just look at this place tonight!" Lanterns were hanging along the porch and around the card tables Jesse and Clint had set up on the lawn. "Your parents use to throw such wonderful parties. Your mother was always thrilled whenever she had even the slightest excuse to host a social gathering."

"Yep." Clint nodded his agreement with that.

"Your father just liked to barbeque. I swear, that man would have tried to grill an entire cow if he could."

Terry nodded. "Hopefully you've inherited some of his skills."

"Yeah, those burgers should be just about ready."

"I'll check on 'em."

Jesse walked beside Clint. "See, I told you this would be fun." He peered at the barbeque grill.

"I suppose."

Felix was standing next to Terry, the two talking about something. Felix was gesturing wildly as he talked, eventually knocking off his brown *Stetson*.

"Pretty much everyone came."

"More than I thought would come." There had to be close to forty people present; five of Clint's neighbours had accepted the invitation.

"They even brought some of their ranch hands along." Jesse was eying one of them as he walked towards the barn.

"That's one of Terry's boys. Steven? Scott? I forget." Clint reached for his beer and took a long swallow. He poked at the burgers.

"He's a hottie." He looked like a younger, more muscular version of his father. Same eyes, same hair, same build, but no comfortably fed stomach as of yet. His legs filled out his snug black jeans.

"He's engaged."

Jesse nodded. "So I've heard," he said sadly.

"You boys hear the news about Danials?" Terry asked as he walked up to join them at the barbeque.

"What news?" Clint asked.

"He's been offered a job in Calgary."

"The constable's transferring?"

"Yeah, in two months time. He'll be gone for a year or so. Felix was just telling me. Off for some new training and a change of scenery."

"Shit." Clint grimaced. "We just got him broken in nicely."

Jesse chuckled at that comment. *I'd like to break him in. So would Clint for that matter.*

"So we're getting another busybody to stick his nose in where he's not wanted."

"Apparently."

Jesse shrugged. "Good for the constable," he said, trying to make his voice sound pleased. "I wonder if his replacement will fill be able to his boots?" *Or his uniform.*

"We can hope so."

"It's not like anything much happens in Nanton. We scarcely need a full-time constable. The town's full of law-abiding folks."

"Most of whom have their own firearms." Jesse grinned.

Jesse looked around the corner of the barn.

The younger man was just zipping up the fly of his black *Wranglers*.

"Sorry to startle you," Jesse said.

"Oh, I was just..." his voice trailed off.

"No problem." Jesse gestured. "There's plenty of room. Steven, right?"

"Scott."

"Jesse." He offered his hand.

Steven stared at him blankly for a moment, and then extended his own.

Jesse took it in a firm grip. "Enjoying yourself?"

"Yes."

"Good to hear." He smiled. *I'm enjoying the view.* A pity he had not been a few moments earlier, and then he might have gotten a better look.

Scott was looking at him a bit sheepishly. "You've got a nice view out here. You and Clint I mean."

"Thanks. It's the same as your farm has. Or close enough."

"No, it's different enough. I should have brought my camera."

"Camera? You take pictures?"

"Well, amateur ones." Scott offered him a friendly smile. "Just of things I like looking at."

"I'd like to see some of your work sometime."

Scott shrugged. "We'll see."

Clint cleared his throat. "I have an announcement."

The gathering fell quiet.

"I've been in town a lot recently, more than most of you can remember." He paused while a few people chuckled. "There's been a reason for it."

Jesse sipped at his beer.

"I've added Jesse to the paperwork for the ranch."

Jesse stared at him in silent shock.

Clint was staring straight at him. "He's worked really hard since he came here and I couldn't have kept the ranch going without him. He's become my best friend...and more.

"He deserves this and I want him to know that."

There was applause from the neighbours.

"Congratulations," Constance said. She patted Jesse on his back.

"I don't know what to say," Jesse said.

"You're a man of property now." Terry belched. "A gentleman."

Everyone laughed.

· Chapter Sixteen

Jesse pulled up the gravel driveway in the Chevy. The Waverly farmhouse looked quiet and the driveway was empty. *Is there anyone home?* He stopped the truck in the driveway—Ted had gotten rid of that loud clattering at last—and he climbed out of the cab. "Hello?" he called out. "There anyone here?"

"Just me." Scott stepped around the corner of the barn. "Afternoon, Jesse." He nodded politely.

"Afternoon, Scott." Jesse smiled warmly at him. "I was just bringing back your mom's dishes. She left them at our place."

"She figured you'd be bringing them back sooner or later. Not that she needs them right away or anything."

"Well, I thought that she might need them so here I am." Jesse knew that he was staring openly at the twenty-five year old. *But I can't help myself.* Scott was wearing just a tight pair of black jeans with his dark brown boots and his broad chest was smooth and muscular. He had a square jawed face with short dark hair. *Yep, he's even hotter than he was the other night.*

"Mom's in town working at some Church social. You can put the dishes in the house. I've got some work to do in here." He hooked his thumb at the barn. "Dad left me some chores before he left."

"There's always chores on the farm, or so Clint tells me." Jesse grinned at the other man. "Don't let me stop you."

"Okay, Jesse." Scott nodded to him, then turned around and walked back into the barn.

He's got a really nice ass. Jesse tore his eyes away from the denim-covered butt cheeks and gave himself a mental shake. *Behave yourself. What would Clint say?* He opened the cab door and reached for the box of dishes.

"I left the dishes on the table." Jesse stepped around the corner of the barn and stopped. *I knew I could hear him working back here.* "I guess I'll be heading off them."

Scott was shoveling cattle feed from the back of an old blue Ford into hoppers for winter storage.

"That looks like quite a job."

"It is." Scott stopped to wipe sweat from his brow. "Dad's a hardworking farmer and with no time for slackers and idlers. He doesn't believe in idle hands."

"I guess not." Jesse shook his head. There was a lot of grain to be moved. *And only him to do it?* "He did leave you a lot."

"He wants it done today."

"Today?"

"Yeah, well I kind of overslept," Scott said with a rueful grin. "I'm not going to be done before he gets home. Dad won't be too happy about that...but what can you do?"

"Well...I could give you a hand."

"Why would you want to do that? Not that I'm saying no to your offer, Jesse, but still...."

"My own chores are done. I don't mind giving you a hand with yours. That's what neighbours do for each other, right?" His blue eyes twinkled. "You can owe me one."

"All right."

Jesse tugged his pale green t-shirt over his head. "Where's an extra shovel?" he asked with a grin.

"You're sure you don't mind helping me like this?"

"Not at all." Jesse smiled at him. *Being this close to a hunk like you is worth the effort. Mmm.* "There's worse ways to spend the day than this."

"You're a real help, Jesse."

"Not a problem."

Jesse shoveled more quickly. Drips of sweat trickled down his brow and his chest as he tried to distract himself. Unable to help himself, he risked a quick glance at Scott. *Discretely, I hope.*

Then Scott glanced up at Jesse, caught his stare, gave him a twisted leering smile in response, and leaned round so that the bulging front of his own jeans was plainly in view.

Jesse swallowed once. "Sorry." Ashamed and embarrassed, he turned quickly back to the work.

Jesse shoveled quickly, throwing the grain into the hopper, and was only aware of Scott watching when he turned round to wipe his brow on his discarded tee shirt.

Scott was smiling a happy smile. "Carry on," he said as he glanced down at Jesse's own crotch.

Jesse was uncomfortable and self-aware now. *I shouldn't have worn these tight jeans,* he thought grimly as he felt his cock twitch inside his briefs. *I should've kept my shirt on. I shouldn't have stopped in here at all.* Still, he could feel the heat of the other man's stare, feel his eyes travel over him, feel the old familiar thrill of erotic adventure coming on... *No! I've moved on now, no more. I'm with Clint.* He flung three more shovels of grain into the hopper, then sat down, exhausted.

"You feeling okay, Jesse?"

"Yeah, of course. Just pushing myself too damn hard." *Trying to impress a younger guy like some old fool.*

"Take a drink." Scott offered him a full water bottle.

Jesse took it and took a long swallow. "Thanks."

"You've been a huge help. I mean it. I couldn't have gotten all this done without you."

"No problem."

"It's a huge help."

"So, you said take pictures?" Jesse asked, trying to distract himself from staring at the other man as he drank some water.

"Yeah. Got my camera over there." Scott went over and picked it up. "It's nothing much to look at."

"It looks expensive."

"Dad called it a useless toy." Scott shrugged. "Mom bought it for me." He paused. "Jesse, do you mind if I take a photo?"

"Of me?"

"Yeah."

"Sure, I guess." Jesse shrugged.

"Okay, come and stand over here. I want one of you standing against the barn, on a bale."

Jesse nodded. "Okay, guess I can do that." He moved to a bale of straw and sat down. "I feel foolish."

"You don't look foolish. You look fine."

Jesse leaned forward, smiling.

Scott clicked off another picture. He moved closer, getting a shot of Jesse sitting on the bale, taken from below.

Innocent.

"Now draw up one leg, and rest your cheek on it."

Jesse grinned at the direction. "You want a show?" The flaunt and show-off in him was coming alive, and he was enjoying being admired. *But this is far enough*, he thought. *It ends here.*

Scott snapped off a final picture. "How about one last request?"

"Just one?"

Scott spoke almost in a whisper, choosing his words carefully. "Sometimes I photograph special people because I think they are beautiful. I've got a private collection of them...just for me."

"You and the cheerleader squad?"

"Something like that." Scott grinned, then ducked his head nervously. "Jesse, can I take two pictures of you in your...underwear?"

Eyes wide, Jesse stared at him.

"It would mean a lot to me."

Jesse said nothing.

"I'd never show them to another living soul.

"Well...."

"I mean, who would I show them too?" Scott laughed. "Who around here would want to see them?"

"Other than Clint?" Jesse shrugged. *Yeah, he'd never show them to another soul. He can't have me, in the flesh, but I could give him a bit of pleasure in an innocent way.* Scott was risking a lot by being so open with him, and he understood only too well. "All right." Jesse would never say anything about Scott's comments or the bulge in his black *Wranglers* that now signaled so shamelessly, so naturally for him. *I've fawned and lusted after guys too. I know how he feels, how frustrated he must be.*

So it didn't feel the least bit wrong as Jesse slowly unzipped his *Wranglers* and then equally slowly pulled off his jeans.

Scott stared and licked his lips. "Shit." Then he began to eagerly whisper just how he wanted Jesse to pose.

Jesse felt the roughness of the straw against his skin, with just the thin material of his white cotton briefs separating him from total nakedness, and his hungry confident smile as the camera clicked. He felt his cock come alive and swell, his briefs tightening deliciously in anticipation of something more to come.

"You have a really nice, sexy body."

"Thanks...yours is really nice too."

Scott blushed. "I'm not used to hearing that. Not from other guys."

Stepping back, to get a shot of Jesse standing up, he watched more closely.

Jesse was getting a bit carried away now. He stood facing squarely at Scott, then thrust forward his hips, tossed back his hair, and gave a glowering sultry look like the best underwear models.

Click.

"How about this?" Facing away, Jesse pulled one side of his briefs down, until the valley of his bottom was just emerging, and held an arching pose.

Click.

Scott moved in, breathing faster now, and let out a long "Mmmmmmmmm."

Jesse held his pose, pouting, tossing his head back. *I'm really enjoying this. I hope that Scott is.*

That was when Scott's strong arms gripped him, and he began to lay wet, hot kisses on Jesse's neck and chest.

Jesse froze. *Did I give him a signal?* He waited a moment for Scott to back off, to apologize. *But I don't really want him to stop.* The press of the other man's jeans against his bare legs, and his hand traveling gently over his back felt so good. *Okay, just play it cool. He'll stop now, he'll apologize, and we'll be back to normal.* No more temptation.

But Scott gripped him even harder from behind, his arm pulling Jesse closer to him. His kisses intensified to wet licks and slow, tongue-swirling sucks. His other hand ran smoothly down Jesse's sweaty, hairy chest, over his belly, and then fondled the profile of his hardened cock through his briefs.

Shit! This is going too far! Jesse thought.

As Scott' hand slipped beneath his waistband and Jesse felt hot fingers groping at his hared shaft and balls, he abruptly realized that he was helpless, panting hard, and had a horny haze filling his head.

"Shit," Scott whispered. "You're so hard."

"Let go of me." But there was no real strength in Jesse's protest.

Scott didn't listen. He wasn't rushing, perhaps savoring this moment of conquest. The whole afternoon stretching ahead, alone with his young horny friend. As if to hint at his plans, he slowly ground his hips into Jesse, the bulge in the front of his jeans pushing hard against Jesse's buttocks.

They stood like that for what seemed like hours.

His panic over now, a new feeling was rapidly taking over Jesse. "We shouldn't do this," he said aloud. "We should stop. Right now." *But it feels so good*, he thought. *Well, maybe just this once.* He softened, relaxed, stretched out in surrender, and moved gently under Scott's roaming hands and lips.

"Come on." Scott steered him into the gloom of the storage barn's dusty interior. "Strip them off."

As Jesse slid his briefs past his ankles, Scott pushed him backwards, gently laying him back in the straw bales. The sensation of prickly roughness an added stimulation, and Scott's mouth closed greedily over his iron-hard cock

As the sensations flowed through him, Jesse realized that he'd been the one who'd led the other man on. *I posed for his photos; I tempted him beyond his control. He has a right to my body.* "Fuck, Scott."

Scott stopped sucking. "You want it. I know you do." Grinning, he backed away and then unzipped his fly. His fat cock, now free of his *Wranglers*, popped out, straight and sleek, a glint of wetness where the purple meat surged out of his foreskin.

Jesse stared. *It's a beauty.*

Scott licked his lips. "I want to taste you." He dropped to his knees again, sucking slowly, deliberately, working all over it, licking Jesse's balls, teasing his tip with his tongue.

"God, that feels so good." Jesse shuddered. "Oh, fuck."

Scott pulled him roughly onto the straw-covered, dirty concrete floor and they tumbled over each other, Scott finally ending up on top with his tongue working deep in Jesse's mouth, while his shaft slid hot and damp against Jesse's thigh.

Jesse felt the first faint twinges of orgasm, and twisted away.

Covered in dust and straw now, panting hard, Jesse leaned against the bales.

Scott stood up, his cock proud and magnificent. "I've been listening to them talk about you and Clint in town. Everyone knows about you two."

"No one talks about you."

Scott shrugged. "I keep it quiet." He licked his lips. "I've wanted a piece of you for a long time."

Jesse blinked. Scott's cock was now swaying an inch over his face, veins distended, the skin stretched tight over the contours and ridges, a thin drool leaking from the tip. He reached up and touched its hardness.

"Take it. Go ahead."

Jesse's lips parted and he felt the heat of Scott's flesh. He opened his mouth wide, ready to take the sleek, intimate feel of his manhood into his throat.

Suddenly he drew away, pushing Jesse roughly down on to the dirty floor.

"What the—" Jesse's legs were in the air, Scott's face at his crotch, first gently licking and tasting, then hungrily eating feasting on his balls, his crack, the tongue eagerly probing his tight hole, worming its way in and bringing on long-forgotten sensations. *He's getting off on being on charge, showing me who's boss.*

Scott broke off again to fetch something from his jeans pocket.

A condom and some lube? Jesse blinked. *Had he planned this all? Did he carry that stuff everywhere with him?* He smiled, caught up in the moment. *The horny bastard. Just like me.*

"You'll like this." His fingers slapped cool lube coarsely over his slit, then he knelt, a leering grin on his face, and Jesse felt the firm outline of his end nudging against his ass.

It was rough, ill-prepared, forceful, but the feel of dirt and sweat on his body gave an added illicit pleasure to the moment, and the initial sting of his entry soon faded as Jesse loosened up and enjoyed the ecstasy of cock, of sensation deep inside him.

Scott's head was back, his eyes screwed up, all his senses filled by the base thrilling pleasure of the first rush of cock. His first few strokes went deeper each time, till his balls were squeezing against Jesse's buttocks and both men were groaning.

From his prone position, Jesse watched his muscular, taut, dirt-covered body writhe and thrust, his eyes never leaving Scott's face, even as ran his hands over his waist and down to his powerful, twitching buttocks.

Scott had set up a rhythm now, slow, insistent, driving deep inside, his large fat cock forcing a groan from Jesse on each stroke.

"Oh shit yeah!" Jesse lost himself in the waves of pleasure. Rough guy-on-guy sex was never this good.

Scott rammed steadily and slowly, taking his pleasure in a controlled way. His thrusts moved them gradually across the rough, muck-covered floor, pausing only to hold off when he felt his cum rising. "Oh, I needed a good fuck like this," he gasped, "but let's not rush it."

Over the sighs and grunts, the dirty intimate whispers from Scott, Jesse heard another note. The rattle of a truck, getting closer.

Scott froze in mid-thrust, and they both listened.

A door slammed.

"Shit!" Jesse was resigned to being caught. *At least maybe Terry will keep quiet about it. Clint is gonna kill me!.* "Shit!" *Fuck Clint—Terry is gonna kill me for this!*

Terry walked past the barn door. "Scott?" he called out.

Scott stayed completely silent.

Jesse could feel his cock harden and twitch, and his fingers dig painfully into his shoulders. *The danger is firing him up.* "He'll catch us. My truck is out there." In plain sight of anyone walking past.

"So?" Scott asked softly.

Terry walked back to his truck.

Can he see us? Jesse wondered. Their nakedness should be shining out like a guilty beacon. Then a slow, silent thrust signaled that Scott couldn't keep still, the tension was too much. *Was he going to attract the attention of the guy*? "Stop it!" he hissed. "Do you want to be caught?"

Scott's cock twitched again. He was trembling and smiling. A drop of sweat fell from his chin onto his chest.

Jesse twisted away from him in panic, pulling out too fast, painfully, and then scrambled away, now wondering hazily where his jeans were.

Scott was still kneeling there on the floor, frozen, with a crumpled look on his face.

"Scott!" Jesse whispered, urgently. He clambered up, shamefully, to a ledge in the bales. *Do I really think I can hide in here?*

But then a magical sound broke the tension. The engine starting, the truck roaring off.

"See? No problem, Jesse." And Scott, with no further delay, clambered after the other man, his erect cock swaying from side to side. "Now, where were we?" Catching Jesse round the waist, he pushed him down onto all fours and mounted him roughly and almost angrily from behind. His pace was quicker now, shafting steadily, his hands gripping his shoulders and squeezing his buttocks hard.

"Easy!"

Scott didn't listen but the pleasure was back again, redoubled.

"Oh, Scott!"

Scott's hard grip on Jesse's body, and the increased energy of his pumping, told Jesse that he was going for the finish. "I want to see you cum." Scott reached down and pulled Jesse's own erection upright against him, pumping the shaft with quick, hard strokes. "I want to see you cum."

"Christ, I'm close!" It was the trigger point now, not much more effort needed to bring Jesse off. Scott's grip tightened.

His hand moved to the end, working the foreskin, and both men felt their climax approach.

Jesse came hard. "Ohhh fuck!" he gasped. Doubled pleasure now, his ass contracting, squeezing Scott's cock powerfully as his spunk shot into clear air, and he writhed and twisted as the spasms hit. More squirts hitting the straw. Then thicker cum, running over Scott's fingers as he pumped out his load while he twisted and groaned.

"Oh Christ yes!" Scott was in full orgasm now and he stiffened, caught his breath, and groaned desperately. "Fuck!" In a vice-like grip, he pulled Jesse close, his hand slippery with semen and sweat, and fingernails scratched his belly. Deep inside, his shaft was pushed as far up as Jesse could take it, rock-hard and pulsing gently. He strained, breath held, as though lifting a heavy load, then he grunted again as he shot his load.

Jesse slumped down into the straw.

Scott grinned and licked the cum off his fingers and gulped appreciatively.

Drawing apart, neither of them said a word.

Jesse found his briefs and jeans and pulled them over his messy body, still feeling weak at the knees.

Scott zipped himself back up and nodded to the trailer. "We should finish that before Dad comes back." He brushed straw and dust from his jeans.

"Yeah." Jesse shook his head. "Fuck."

Scott picked up his shovel. "You okay, Jesse?"

"Yeah, sure." Jesse staggered over to the other shovel.

They had been shoveling for five minutes when Terry pulled up in his Ford. "So there you are."

"Yep, here we are." Scott kept shoveling.

Jesse nodded his head, trying to ignore the burning in his cheeks. *Matches the one in my ass.*

"You talked Jesse into helping you?"

"He brought Mom's dishes back and volunteered to give me a hand." Scott laughed and winked at Jesse.

"Yeah, I offered to help." Jesse could feel the straw in his hair, the dirt in his back, a faint smear of cum on his belly, the telltale signs of what he had been up too.

"I saw Clint's truck here." Terry walked closer. "Get the job done and then go and clean yourself up," he told his son. "Constance wants us to join her sister in town for supper."

"Sure, Dad." Scott nodded.

Terry gave Jesse another glance, then turned and walked up to the farmhouse.

Jesse rammed the shovel wearily into the pile of grain. *How could I have been so stupid?* he wondered. *When did I become such a mindless slut? Why did I give in so easily to Scott's crude advances?*

He looked up and could feel Scott's stare driving into him, lusting after his just-been-fucked body. The embarrassment burned inside, but deep in his briefs, his cock started to throb and swell.

Chapter Seventeen

Jesse poured himself a mug of coffee. "What was I thinking yesterday?" he asked himself.

Clint had left earlier that morning with Terry to help another neighbour with cattle branding.

"'I'm not trained for it,' he said. 'I'd just be in the way.'" Jesse sighed. "At least Terry didn't say anything to him on the phone." *I hope.* He pushed the kitchen door open and stepped outside.

A clear blue sky arched over the prairie. No clouds marred the pristine beauty.

Jesse yawned, his mouth open wide enough that he thought his jaw might not close again. *Clint wondered why I spent the night tossing and turning so restlessly. If he only knew....*

"Shit, what I was thinking?" Jesse kicked at a clod of dirt with his boot. "I've got a good thing going here with Clint so why am I trying to screw it all up?" At least Clint had been out when Jesse had come home. *I had time to shower and clean up before he got back. He doesn't need to know.* "It won't happen again."

He finished his coffee.

* * *

A shiny navy blue station wagon pulled up the drive.

Jesse stepped out of the barn as he heard the car's motor. He hooked his hands into the pockets of his jeans and leaned against the barn.

A man dressed in black jeans, black shirt, and black hat got out of the car. "Good morning, Jesse."

"Morning, Cecil." Jesse nodded to the country vet. "Good to see you again. Nothing serious going I hope. I haven't heard any more reports about mad cows or foot-and-mouth recently."

"No, nothing like that around here. I'm just out making the rounds." Cecil Latimer had a rugged face, with a ready smile for the people he visited. "Clint around?"

"He's off helping with the branding."

"Ah, of course. I should have remembered that was happening today. Slipped my mind though. Guess that means I must be getting old." Cecil gestured to the barn. "All the animals are well?"

"Yep. I was just getting Misty saddled up. Got some chores to take care of."

"There's always chores on a farm."

"That there are."

"I won't keep you long then." He paced towards the barn. "I'll just check on the horses and then I'll be gone."

"Take all the time you need." Jesse shrugged. "The chores will keep."

"That they will." Felix smiled and nodded. "That they will." He paused in mid-step. "I hear that congratulations are in order for you."

"Are they?"

"I heard that Clint's made you the partial owner of this place."

"Clint would say that some folks around town have big mouths."

"No, Clint would say something more like 'A man's got no privacy to take a shit without folks talking.'"

Jesse laughed aloud. "Yeah, that sounds more like Clint."

Cecil emerged from the barn. "They all seem healthy enough."

"Good to hear."

"You should be pleased with yourselves. I think you and Clint have the healthiest horses in the area."

"I'll be sure to let Clint know that."

"Good." Cecil got into his car and put the key into the ignition. The motor ground.

"Damn." Cecil popped the hood and climbed out of the wagon. "Stupid thing needs to go the garage."

Jesse shook his head. "Something serious?"

"Just a loose connection I think." Cecil leaned in to look at the engine.

"I'm pretty clueless when it comes to cars. Had a few friends try to teach me about them, but...." Jesse stared. *When he bends over, his ass isn't half bad.* He blinked at his thoughts.

"Look at this." Cecil motioned Jesse to come closer and have a look at the problem so the younger man obediently bent over next to him to look in the engine. "There's a tear in this hose I think." He pointed to a hose. "I'll have to rig something cover it. Air's getting in and choking the motor."

Jesse was looking.

"Can you see it?"

"No..."

"It's right about here." Cecil took Jesse's hand and guided it to the hose reaching under to feel the tear.

Jesse took a deep breath. *What the hell am I feeling?* he wondered with some shock. The vet was easily twenty years his senior...but there was still a stirring in his jeans. Standing upright, he felt very self-conscious of the growing bulge in his crouch. *What the hell?* He could not help but take a quick peek at Cecil—and the vet had a bulge in his own crotch. *I must be seeing things.*

"I'll just need your help to fix it." Cecil hurried to the trunk and dug out a roll of silvery duct tape. "It fixes everything."

"So what do you need me to do?"

"Just hold that hose like this." He guided Jesse's hands into position. "And then flex it just so."

"I think I can handle that." Jesse took a deep breath and willed his cock to be still. Bent under the car's hood means lots more close quarter body contact and he quickly got hard all over again. *Think about Clint, he told himself. Or even Sally for that matter.*

"Damn, this is being a bugger." After some manoeuvring, they found the only way they could do it was with Cecil semi-crouched at the front of my car and Jesse right behind him, bending over on top of him.

Jesse felt himself close to laughter. *We're in the exact position as if I were fucking him up the ass.* There was no way to hide the growing erection poking in his butt cheek. *Christ, what's he gonna say*? Jesse could not really see what Cecil was doing, which made it tricky to hold the hose right.

Cecil kept shifting around, so that Jesse's cock kept jabbed him somewhere else in the ass, eventually settling with it resting in the groove right between his cheeks.

Christ, I feel so embarrassed. "Sorry if my cell phone is poking you in the ass like that."

"Is it?" Cecil shifted again and seemed to stick his butt out so my cock jabbed even harder. Then he moved forward providing a little space between them.

"Sorry," Jesse said as he let his hands slipped and the hose flopped into position.

"Don't worry, Jesse, I finished a little while ago." He gave Jesse a smile. "That should be enough to get me going."

Jesse stared blankly at him.

Cecil slammed the hood and then climbed behind the wheel and turned the key. The motor roared to life. "Thank you."

"Uh, no problem." Jesse was not sure what to say.

"See you later." Cecil waved and pulled off down the driveway.

"What the fuck just happened here?" Jesse asked himself.

* * *

Misty neighed softly.

Jesse patted the light grey mare's neck with a few soft words.

Riding the fences was not a glamorous job, but it had to be done every few weeks to check for broken rails or breaks.

"This isn't what I expected out of life," he said aloud. The fall wind was cold, blowing off the Rockies and he huddled down inside his denim jacket until it passed.

Misty plodded along.

"Back in Lethbridge, hell, back in Redcliff, I used to dream about being a cop," he mused aloud. "Cops always got me excited...even before I knew why I was getting hot. Seeing a hot hunk in a police officer's uniform was great.

"Course, every boy dreams about being a cop or a fireman. Why would I be any different? But I never saw myself working in a store.

"I wanted more out of life. I never saw myself working a farm

The sun slipped behind a cloud.

"And here I am, part owner of this place. A man of property." He gave his head a shake, and then adjusted his hat. "Now I have a reason to work hard out here. This place is mine."

And that made a difference.

"There's a beauty to this farm. The land is rugged, and so is Clint." He frowned. "I never thought I'd meet a guy like Clint." There was no doubt about it in his mind—Clint was the reason he was staying. "He changed my life. Things are better out here...better than living back home with my family and their religion. It's better than living in Calgary and labouring in the oil fields.

"*This* is where I want to be."

He patted Misty's neck. "Enough of this, girl. Let's head home."

Jesse turned back towards the farmhouse.

Also by Frank Sol

Novels Of The Sensual City
A Family Affair

Novels On The Prairies
Bareback Range
Return To Bareback Range
Fenced In

9 798223 429715